Benjamin Brodie

Autobiography of the late Sir Benjamin C. Brodie

Second Edition

Benjamin Brodie

Autobiography of the late Sir Benjamin C. Brodie
Second Edition

ISBN/EAN: 9783337013981

Printed in Europe, USA, Canada, Australia, Japan

Cover: Foto ©Raphael Reischuk / pixelio.de

More available books at **www.hansebooks.com**

SIR BENJAMIN C. BRODIE,

BART.

AUTOBIOGRAPHY

OF THE LATE

SIR BENJAMIN C. BRODIE,

BART.

SECOND EDITION.

LONDON:

LONGMANS, GREEN, AND CO.

1865.

PREFACE.

THE following Memoir was found among my
father's papers. It bears marks of having been
primarily intended for the benefit of those
most immediately connected with him. Yet it
contains so much of special interest to the
members of his own profession, and such careful
sketches of many persons distinguished in it as
to whom he had the fullest means of forming
a correct judgment, that it appeared unreason-
able to withhold it from publication. There is
also much of wider interest in such a record
of the career of an eminent professional man.
It must be profitable to many to learn how
he was educated, and by what genuine work

he won his way to the rewards which the public bestows. Also, in thus fully tracing his course in life, I cannot but believe that my father had reference to the encouragement and support which his example would afford to any who hereafter should find themselves in the position which he once occupied at the commencement of an arduous and responsible profession, from which they feel tempted to shrink as almost beyond their strength.

B. C. B.

Oxford: *March* 8, 1865.

AUTOBIOGRAPHY

SIR BENJAMIN BRODIE,

BART.

———◆———

I KNOW but little of my father's family. My paternal grandfather was, I believe, born in Banffshire, somewhere about the year 1710 or 1711. He came to London a very humble adventurer, having, as there was reason to believe, been involved (in those days of Jacobitism) in some political trouble. He married a daughter of Dr. Peter Shaw, a physician, and first cousin of another Dr. Shaw, who was an eminent medical practitioner, and whose daughter married the first Dr. Warren. Dr. Peter Shaw had followed the fortunes of the Stuarts, and, if I am not mistaken, had accompanied King James II. abroad. My grandfather is described by Dr. Denman, who married one of his daughters, as an army clothier; but he also had some post in the Stamp Office, which fact I have learned from some letters which I have in my possession of my father's to his sisters, addressed under cover to my grandfather to save the postage.

My father scarcely ever spoke of his own family, and what little I know of them is chiefly derived from my unmarried aunt, Margaret Brodie. The supposition that my grandfather had become involved in some political difficulties is rather confirmed by the circumstance of his having married afterwards the daughter of a staunch Jacobite, and by the Jacobite songs which my before-mentioned aunt was accustomed to repeat to us when I was a child. The only relations with whom he kept up any communication were a naval Captain, I believe afterwards Admiral, Brodie, who, as my aunt used to report to us, had two very handsome sons, and Mr. Brodie, of Brodie, who held the office of Lord Lyon. From his connection with the latter, I conclude that we are of the family of Brodie of Brodie. Of his own immediate family I know nothing, except that after his death two of his nephews came to London, apparently knowing nothing about him, on the speculation that there might be something for them to inherit, departing, however, at once on finding that he had left a family, and that there was nothing for them : being never heard of afterwards.

My paternal grandmother had the reputation of being a person of very considerable abilities, and I have formerly seen some of her manuscripts which seemed to prove that this was really the case. My aunt used to boast that we had somehow royal blood in our veins (that of the Plantagenets), an honour which my friend Charles Edward Long has shown to be shared by many thousand persons of various grades, from princes and dukes down to cobblers and carpenters.

My father was educated on the foundation at the Charterhouse, and afterwards at Worcester College, Oxford. As a boy he was patronized by the first Lord Holland. and passed much of

his time at Holland House.   On leaving the
University he took holy orders, and it seems
from some letters of his which I have in my
possession, that at one period he held a curacy
at Adderbury, in Oxfordshire.   He remained
there, however, only for a short time, and when
Stephen the second Lord Holland purchased an
estate and mansion at Winterslow in Wiltshire
of one of the Thistlethwayte family, he rented
a cottage in the same place in order that he
might be near him.   From his letters to his
sisters written at this period, it appears that he
lived almost constantly with Lord Holland, to
whom, as well as his brother Charles James Fox,
he was sincerely attached, always speaking of
them (especially of the former) even to the last
days of his life with the greatest affection.

Lord Holland died in 1774, having directed
in his will that my father should have offered to
him the presentation of the first of three livings
which he had in his gift which should become
vacant.   The vacancy soon occurred in consequence of the death of the Rev. Dr. Thistlethwayte, the incumbent of Winterslow, and thus

my father became the rector of the parish in which he had previously resided.

In the year 1775 my father married one of the daughters of Mr. Collins, of Milford, a banker at Salisbury. They had six children, four sons and two daughters, and I was their fourth child, having been born in the year 1783.

My earliest recollections carry me back to the Rectory at Winterslow. They are still as vivid as ever, and even now my dreams continually present to me these scenes of my early life.

My father was altogether remarkable for his talents and acquirements. He was well acquainted with general literature, and was an excellent Latin and Greek scholar for the period in which he lived, when a critical knowledge of the Greek language was not so far advanced as it is at the present time. He was endowed with a large share of energy and activity; but looking back at this early period of my life, I cannot doubt that he was a disappointed person. In the beginning of his career he had reason to expect that he would rise high in his profession; and there is little doubt that his expectations would have been realized if Mr. Fox had continued longer in power. As it was, his first preferment was his last. He paid great attention to the duties of his parish, and knew every one of the seven hundred or eight hundred individuals belonging to it. But besides this he attended more than any one of the neighbouring gentry to the public business of our part of Wilt-shire, as a magistrate and deputy-lieutenant, and in other ways. Thus he acquired a considerable local influence beyond that which with his moderate fortune he would have acquired otherwise.

He held what is commonly called a very good living; and my mother, not many years after her marriage, inherited a fortune of 10,000l. as her share of her father's fortune; to which ultimately there was an addition of some thousands of pounds from other parts of her family. My father was very anxious that his sons should be well educated. But with his means he found that he could not afford to send us all to public schools; and as he did not like to send us to schools of an inferior order, he determined, in addition to his other undertakings, to instruct us himself. For many years this was indeed the principal object of his life, and I cannot too strongly express my gratitude for the thought and labour which he bestowed on the cultivation of our minds.

My elder sister, who afterwards married the Rev. Mr. Marsh, chancellor of the diocese of Salisbury, was educated with her brothers. She was well acquainted with Greek and Latin, and afterwards instructed her own children in those languages previously to their being sent to West-minster School. Being seven years my senior, she took some part in the instruction of myself also. When I was seven years old, my father being for a time absent from home, she super-intended my first translations of Ovid, and some six years afterwards I went through Euclid's Elements with her assistance.

Our life at Winterslow was removed as far as possible from one of idleness. In the summer my brothers and myself rose at six o'clock, and two hours were devoted to study (generally learning to repeat Greek and Latin poetry, or Cicero's

Orations) before we breakfasted at half-past eight o'clock. Immediately after breakfast we resumed our studies; we dined at three o'clock, and were then at our studies again from four to six o'clock. In the winter our hours of study were somewhat different; and from eight to half-past nine o'clock in the evening my father read some book of amusement or instruction aloud to the whole family. On two days in the week when my father was absent on public business, we had half-holidays. We had no other vacations during the whole year, except on some grand occasions, such as a cricket match, or the first few days of the skating season. On the whole, our average time of study was from seven to eight hours daily; and there having been only very rare intermissions, the result has been that the habit of being employed in some kind of study became a part and parcel of my nature. Idleness even for a single day has been always irksome to me, and I have had little inclination for any pursuit which did not seem to lead to some ulterior object. Much of my success in my worldly career is, I am convinced, to be attributed to this discipline in my early years.

Being a large family we had a society among ourselves ; and only a very limited acquaintance with the families in the neighbourhood. Indeed there were but few for us to visit. The nearest place at which we could have any acquaintance was Salisbury, and this was by the carriage road seven miles distant. Some of our cousins, however, used to come at times to stay with us for a few weeks. Among them were the present Lord Denman, the present Sir George Staunton, Colonel Squire of the Royal Engineers, who afterwards died in the Peninsula, and his two brothers. Lord Denman resided with us as a pupil of my father's for a year after leaving Eton. Referring to him at this period, I cannot but recognise in him the same character which he has preserved through life. He was a thoroughly good boy, upright and honourable as he has been ever since. As we grew older we formed other acquaintance, and I may mention specially Mr. (afterwards Dr.) Maton, who afterwards became a physician of great eminence in the metropolis ; Mr. (now Sir John) Stoddart, who for many years filled the office of chief justice at Malta; and the late Mr. Wray, of the Chancery bar. These were ever afterwards my most intimate friends. At the present time the only one of these who remains among us is Sir John Stoddart, still retaining an active and vigorous intellect, and engaged in literary pursuits at nearly eighty years of age.

There were undoubtedly disadvantages belonging to the kind of life which my brothers and myself led at this period, having so little acquaintance with those of our own age and station. We had much to learn when we came into the world which others learn as boys at Eton or Harrow or Rugby. In my own case, one was a shyness in general society, which for a long time was very oppressive, and which it took many years for me to overcome; and another was that, not having sufficient opportunities of comparing myself with others, I formed no right estimate of my own character, overrating myself in some things, and underrating myself in others. Yet I am inclined to think

that what we gained in some respects was fully
equal to what we lost in others. In my solitary
walks through Lord Holland's woods, or over
the Wiltshire downs, I early acquired the habit
of reflection, and of thinking and judging for myself, and the consequence has been that through
the whole of the after part of my life I have
never been inclined to adopt opinions on the
authority of others, nor until I had looked at
both sides of the question. I also learned to
be independent of others for occupation and
amusement, and of this I have felt the great
advantage ever since. In the many years previous to my marriage, during which I was climbing up-hill in my profession, when I passed what
is called the empty season in London, with very
few of my acquaintance left in the great city,
time never hung heavily on my hands. Indeed very few portions of my life have been
much happier than those in which I had no
other society than that of my books and writings,
and little recreation beyond that of a solitary
walk in the evening in the fields which now
form the Regent's Park, or those which are now

covered with houses and gardens in the district of St. John's Wood.

Notwithstanding what I have said as to our want of society at Winterslow, we were not altogether without opportunities of studying the characters of others, and of learning how to deal with mankind. Education and position in society modify our tastes and sentiments and habits, but they do not alter the essential qualities of human nature, the observation of which in one class of persons cannot fail to teach us much of what we want to know as to others.   In the year 1798, when there was an alarm on account of a supposed probability of invasion by the French, my elder brothers and myself raised a company of volunteers, amounting at last to as many as 140 in number.   The eldest of us was only nineteen years of age, and I myself was not more than fourteen, when, through my father's influence, we received our commissions as captain, lieutenant, and ensign.   The men were clothed and armed by Government, and received pay for each day of exercise.   We expended the pay which we received as officers in one way or another on the corps, principally in giving them entertainments in my father's great barn, after being inspected by the general officer of the district (or on some other occasions), to which we invited some of our friends in the neighbourhood and the farmers of our parish. I have no doubt that the pay and the dinners did much for us; still, as we were nothing but volunteers in the true sense of the word, and as each one of our soldiers could go and come as he pleased, if we had not attended to their feelings, and thus exercised an influence over them, we could never have maintained among them the necessary discipline, nor have kept up the number of our corps. I cannot look back at these boyish occupations without being satisfied that they afforded me many useful lessons by which I profited in the world afterwards. I may add that we bestowed great pains on the drilling of our corps; and, by diligently studying the system of tactics published by authority, we succeeded in obtaining for it the credit of being by far the best disciplined of any in our part of the country.

In the year 1799 my elder brother, Peter, left Winterslow to be entered at the Temple and reside as a law-student in London. My next brother, William, was at this time residing at Salisbury, it being intended that he should be brought up to the woollen cloth manufactory, for which Salisbury had in those times a reputation, which it has long since lost. In the latter part of the year 1801 I followed my elder brother to London. This interval of two years from 1799 to 1801 was a very important portion of my life. I was old enough to know that I must depend on myself for making my way in the world, and that I might never again have the same opportunity of laying in a store of general knowledge. I read a great deal of Greek and Latin, and still more in other subjects. In mathematics I never soared higher than geometry and algebra, but of these I learned enough to obtain a sufficient knowledge of mechanics, optics, and hydrostatics for ordinary purposes, and a general knowledge of astronomy. In general literature my reading was very various, including many books which might as well have been left to a later period : such as Locke's 'Essay on the Understanding ;' Harris's 'Philosophical Essays ;' Reid's 'Inquiry ;' Priestley's 'Abridgment of Hartley's Theory ;' Godwin's 'Political Justice ;' Smith's 'Theory of the Moral Sentiments ;' &c. I also acquired some knowledge of chemistry. I knew Lavoisier's 'Elements' by heart, and fitted up a laboratory with such simple apparatus as with my very limited means I was able to make or purchase. I read a great deal of English poetry, and some French and Italian. What I had then committed to memory of Greek and Latin and English poets has been a great resource to me since, during the many long nights which I travelled by myself in a postchaise, before the invention of railways. But I cannot say that my poetical taste at that time was of the purest kind. I was a vast admirer of Darwin, and never properly appreciated Shakespeare until I had lived for some few years in the world. Looking back at these two years, the impression on my mind is that it would have been well if I had read less and digested more ; nevertheless I am satisfied that they have been to me of the greatest value, and that if they could have been blotted out of my existence, my position in society would at the present time have been very different from what it really is.

My two elder brothers being away, and my third brother being several years younger than myself, the result was that during the two years of which I have just spoken, I was thrown more into the society of my father than at any former period. He had been a very strict disciplinarian, and the respect and affection which I had for him had been mixed up with no small portion of fear. But it was now much otherwise. I became to a considerable extent his companion. In the early part of the day I read with him some Latin and Greek works—generally the latter. In the afternoon and evening he left me very much to pursue my studies in my own way. Between our morning occupations and dinner-time, when I was not engaged in some business relating to our volunteer corps, and he was not engaged by his duties as a magistrate and deputy-lieutenant, which at this time were considerable, I accompanied him in his walks. Allowing for the difference of more than forty years in our ages, our tastes were a good deal similar, so that my attentions were not paid to him merely as a matter of duty. My father, as I have already mentioned, was a man of great natural talent, and had a very cultivated mind; and the fact of my being much in his society made me feel as if I was an older person than I really was, and in part explains how it happens that, when I went forth into the world afterwards, my sympathies were much more with those who were beyond myself in years than with those of my own age. Other circumstances, however, contributed to produce the same result. I have already referred to Robert Wray as one of my early acquaintance. He was the son of a gentleman of independent fortune at Salisbury, about five years my senior, and of a very thoughtful and reflecting turn of mind. There was a close intimacy between us, which terminated only with his death. Thus, being thrown a good deal on my own resources, I was constrained to seek amusement for my leisure hours, not in the usual pursuit of boys,

but in my father's library, picking up many
scraps of knowledge, which I have found to be
far from useless since.   To those who may take
the trouble of looking at these manuscripts hereafter, all this may appear very trifling and egotistical; but the truth is, that I feel an interest
in looking back at these circumstances in my
early life which had an influence on my tastes
and habits afterwards; and it may be that something of the same kind of interest will be felt
by my wife and children when I am taken from
them.

As long as I can remember anything, my father
always endeavoured to impress on our minds
that we should have to obtain our livelihood by
our own exertions; that he would do his utmost
to give us a good education, to accustom us to
industrious habits, and to put us in the way of
providing for ourselves, but that he could do
nothing more.   We supposed that he left us to
choose our professions for ourselves, but the fact
was, as I now believe, that, without our being
aware of it, he himself directed our inclinations.

My elder brother became a lawyer, and has since obtained the highest place in his profession as a conveyancing barrister, distinguished alike for his legal knowledge, his integrity, and his accuracy. My next brother, three years older than myself, as I have already mentioned, was first engaged in the woollen cloth manufactory at Salisbury. This, however, soon became a failing business, the Salisbury manufacturer, after the introduction of steam, being unable to compete with those of the coal districts. Some years afterwards, however, he succeeded on the death of one of my maternal uncles to a very lucrative business, which had been for some generations in my mother's family, and by which my grandfather had been enabled to accumulate a considerable fortune, became the proprietor of a provincial newspaper, and a banker. He married a niece of Mr. Hussey, who represented Salisbury in Parliament, with a good fortune; and was for many years a most prosperous person, living in the best society of that part of the country. In an evil hour he was persuaded to aspire to a seat in the House of Commons. He

was elected for Salisbury by a large majority;
was re-elected after two pretty hard contests;
and kept his seat until, after the sudden death
of a managing clerk in whom he had placed a
too unlimited confidence, he was led to accept
the Chiltern Hundreds.

As to myself, it was determined that I should
embark in some part of the medical profession.
Dr. Denman had married one of my father's
sisters.   Dr. Baillie and Sir Richard Croft had
married my first cousins.   The great reputation
which they had respectively acquired perhaps
led my father to give my mind this direction,
and disposed me to be easily guided according
to his wishes.   However that may have been,
in the autumn of 1801 I was sent to London,
and there entered on those pursuits which have
been the chief object of my life.

Others have often said to me that they supposed that I must have had, from the first,
a particular taste or liking for my profession.
But it was no such thing; nor does my experience lead me to have any faith in those special
callings to certain ways of life which some

young men are supposed to have. For the most part, these are mere fancies, which are liable to give way to other fancies with as little reason as they themselves first began to exist. Such persons take the *ignotum pro magnifico*; and when they find that the *magnificum* is not equal to their expectations, they as readily fly to something else. The persons who succeed best in professions are those who, having (perhaps from some accidental circumstance) been led to embark in them, persevere in their course as a matter of duty, or because they have nothing better to do. They often feel their new pursuit to be unattractive enough in the beginning; but as they go on, and acquire knowledge, and find that they obtain some degree of credit, the case is altered; and from that time, they become every day more interested in what they are about. There is no profession to which these observations are more applicable than they are to the medical. The early studies are, in some respects, disagreeable to all, and to many repulsive. But in the practical exercise of its duties in the hospital, there is much that is of the highest interest; and the collateral sciences, to those whose position gives them the opportunity of cultivating them, offer at least as much to gratify our curiosity and excite our admiration as any other branches of knowledge, not even excepting the sublime investigations of astronomy.

When I first came as an adventurer to London, I knew as little as possible of the profession for which I was destined, and I had to grope my way in it as well as I could by myself. I soon found that I could not be a physician without a University degree. My father had sent none of us to Oxford or Cambridge. I do not certainly know why he did not do so; for although, with his family of six children, his pecuniary means were limited, we were far beyond ordinary schoolboys in our knowledge of Greek and Latin; and I have known many much inferior to ourselves, as to these studies, who were able to obtain exhibitions such as, with what he could have done for us, would have enabled us to obtain an academical education, and put us in the way of rising in the University afterwards. I suspect that for these ancient seats of learning, as they were then constituted, he had no very great respect, and that he feared that we might there lose those habits of persevering industry which he had been at so great pains to give us.

During my first season in London, I attended Mr. Abernethy's lectures on Anatomy. He was an admirable teacher. He kept up our attention so that it never flagged, and that what he told us could not be forgotten. He did not tell us so much as some other lecturers; but what he did, he told us well. His lectures were full of original thought, of luminous and almost poetical illustrations, the tedious details of descriptive anatomy being occasionally relieved by appropriate and amusing anecdotes, which, though they had been repeated over and over again, as one course succeeded another, were very agreeable to us new-comers. Like most of his pupils, I was led to look up to him as a being of a superior order, and I could conceive nothing better than to follow in his footsteps; and thus I was led to regard the department of the profession to which he belonged as that to which I should belong myself. Of this conclusion I have never since had reason to repent ; and after an experience of fifty years, I am confirmed in the opinion that the pursuit of what is called pure surgery, such as it is in large cities, in connection with a hospital and a medical school, is more replete with interest, and, on the whole, more satisfactory, than any of the other branches into which the *ars medendi* is divided.

Although I never even dreamed of retracing my steps, nor allowed myself to think that I could venture to do so, it must be confessed that there was much which tended to damp my ardour in the beginning. A very few days were sufficient to overcome the disgust occasioned by my first entry into the dissecting-room ; but the study of bones and muscles and bloodvessels was far from being attractive in the first instance, after the very different studies in which I had been previously engaged. Now, in the theatre and the dissecting-room, I felt, though with numbers around me, like a solitary person.

Between myself and the great majority of the students there was nothing in common. In a medical school, indeed, there is a great mixture of persons. There is always a certain number of well-educated young men. But these are a minority. The effect of the absurd system of apprenticeship to an apothecary—which custom formerly, and since that an Act of Parliament, has imposed on what are called general practitioners—is that the great mass of students are sadly deficient in this respect. If I spoke on subjects in which I was interested, they did not understand me, neither did I understand them. There were only two among them with whom I had much acquaintance: one of them a young physician of the name of Crawford, a nephew of Crawford who wrote on animal heat, and who died not very long afterwards; and the other was Lawrence, who has since acquired so large and well-deserved a reputation. The latter was, even then, a remarkable person. I never knew any one who had a greater capacity for learning than he had, nor more industry, nor who at the same age had a greater amount of information, not merely on matters relating to his future profession, but on a great variety of other subjects.

From that time to the present, Lawrence and myself have been moving in parallel lines, he having had the largest share of private practice next to myself; and it may be regarded as somewhat to the credit of both of us that there has never been any manifestation of jealousy between us. I have already mentioned that, when a young man, he had some faculties in great perfection, and he has them still, but little (as far as I can see) impaired by the addition of fifty years to his age. He has a great memory, and can readily recur to, and make use of, what he knows. He has considerable powers of conversation, but without obtruding himself to the exclusion of others, as is the case with too many of those who are reputed to be good talkers. What he says is full of happy illustrations, with, at times, a good deal of not ill-natured sarcasm. In public speaking, he is collected, has great command of language, and uses it correctly, but not equal to what he is in the ordinary intercourse of society. In writing, his style is pure, free from all affectation, yet in general not sufficiently concise. His reading has been extensive; he is well acquainted with modern, and moderately so with the ancient, languages. His professional writings contain a vast deal of information, but it is more as to what he has taken from other authors than as to the results of his own experience and observation. That he is thoroughly acquainted with his profession cannot be doubted, for it would not have been possible for him otherwise to retain for so long a period the high place which he has occupied.

If I had but few associates among my fellow-students in the medical school, I was fortunate in those whom I had at the same time out of it.

My elder brother was in London studying for the Bar, and he and I lodged together at a house in Carey Street, Lincoln's Inn. Denman, my first cousin, was studying the law also, and had chambers in Lincoln's Inn. Merivale, with whom I was acquainted as a friend of Denman, and as having been a visitor at my father's house in

Wiltshire, and who was afterwards well known for his literary acquirements, and especially as the author of the translations of the Greek Anthology, was engaged in the same pursuit, and residing also in Lincoln's Inn. Besides these, I was on intimate terms with other law students, among them Wray, with whom I had previously associated in Wiltshire; Stoddart, already mentioned as a former friend, who, after having been leading the life of a literary man, was then studying for the Bar of Doctors' Commons; Gifford (Lord Gifford afterwards), and one whose name was Barwis, who, not being very successful at the Bar, became afterwards the Marquis of Ormonde's agent in Ireland, and continued to be one of my best and kindest friends to the end of his days. To these I may add Dr. Maton, whom I had known in my earlier days, and whom, while I was a boy, I had sometimes accompanied in his botanical excursions. He had then lately begun to practise as a physician in London; rising afterwards to be one of the principal physicians in the west end of the town. All of these whom I have mentioned were several years older than myself, and I hold it to be one of the greatest advantages which I have had in life, that I was thus at an early age thrown into the society of intelligent and well-conducted persons, whose minds were more matured than my own.

Dr. Maton and some of his friends, while at Oxford, had formed themselves into a society for the discussion of literary and other subjects. The objects of the society were innocent enough, and one of their rules was to exclude all questions connected with religion and politics. But in those days, when the French Revolution was going on, and parties were reckless and violent at home, it excited the jealousy of the authorities of the University, who insisted on it being put an end to. When several of the founders of it met afterwards in London, they agreed to re-establish it under the name of the Academical Society, and it accordingly assembled once in a week at apartments at a large house in Bell Yard, between Lincoln's Inn and the Temple. Dr. Maton was its president, and through his kindness, youngster as I was, I was elected a

member of it. Here, besides some of my friends
already mentioned, I met with several persons
who have since become much distinguished in
their several ways : Lord Glenelg, and his brother Robert, who died afterwards while Governor
of Madras ; Bowdler, Francis Horner, Dr. Bateman (author of the work on ' Cutaneous Diseases '), Sir Henry Ellis, and others. Not long
after I had joined the society, a young Scotch-
man of uncouth appearance was admitted into
it, whom very few of us knew, who at that time,
while a student of one of the Inns of Court, was
maintaining himself, as I believe, by reporting
for the newspapers. I remember that he read
an essay, the object of which was to prove that
war had been the great agent in civilising the
world. He was an indifferent speaker, but what
he said was always to the purpose. This un-
known person became afterwards Attorney-General, then Lord Chancellor of Ireland, and is
now the Lord Chief Justice Campbell. The
three best speakers were the two Grants and
Bowdler. The latter, if he had lived, would undoubtedly have occupied a considerable place in

society; but he had ill-health, and died a very few
years after the period of which I am now speaking. I was too shy and too much awed by the
society of persons generally a good deal older
than myself to take any part in the debates, except when it was my turn to open the discussion,
and on these occasions my speeches had little to
recommend them, except their brevity. In the
first year, however, I furnished an essay on the
advantages which might be derived from metaphysical enquiries. I read other essays afterwards, one on the principles of science, and the
mode of conducting scientific enquiries (which
gained me some credit in the society), and
another on what were supposed to be modern
discoveries, which could be found in Pliny's
'Natural History.' I mention these trifling
matters merely because they show that, although
I was really studying hard in my profession, I
nevertheless found some leisure to think of other
things. Ellis and myself were for some time
joint secretaries, or, as we were called, registrars
of the society, and hence arose an intimacy between us, which has continued uninterrupted to

the present day.   He was then a sub-librarian
of the British Museum, of which institution
he has been now for many years the principal
official person.

As I have introduced the 'Academical Society,' I shall give the rest of its history, which
may, however, be comprised in a few words. The
most zealous of its members was our president
Dr. Maton.   He regarded it as an institution
for the advancement of literary and scientific
knowledge, and, I have no doubt, looked for-
ward to the time when it would occupy a high
place among the learned societies of the metropolis.   But it was too near to the Inns of Court
for this purpose.   The young lawyers especially
were wont to introduce political allusions, on
which occasion Maton, sitting as president,
would take off the three-cornered hat which he
wore according to the fashion of that day, and
warn them that this was contrary to our regu-
lations.   But his warnings were gradually less
and less attended to: the society assumed more
and more the character of a common debating
club, and our president resigned. The meetings

were afterwards transferred to a larger room in Chancery Lane, and, I believe, flourished very much in their new character for a few years, then declined, and died a natural death. In fact, the altered habits of society have not been favourable to these evening meetings. In the beginning of the century lawyers dined at half-past four or five o'clock, and had long evenings. In like manner the Royal Society Club dined at the Crown and Anchor at five o'clock, and made a full attendance at Somerset House afterwards. But now, when few persons of the best educated classes dine before seven o'clock, the meetings of the Royal Society are scarcely attended, there being not unfrequently no more than twenty or thirty of the Fellows present, or, as the French say, *assisting* on these occasions.

During my first winter in London, I attended Mr. Abernethy's lectures on anatomy, and worked in the dissecting-room, and attended Dr. (now Sir Alexander) Crichton's lectures on chemistry every other morning. My time was not so much occupied but that I had leisure for some other pursuits. I read the first volume of

D

Dugald Stewart's 'Moral Philosophy,' which was then lately published, and Berkeley's 'Dialogues' and 'Principles of Human Knowledge,' which last I obtained for the sum of half-a-crown at a bookstall. If I were called upon to name the author from a perusal of whose works I have derived the most advantage, I should mention Berkeley. Of course I refer not to his hypothesis of the non-existence of the material universe, but to the example which he affords of clear, precise, and accurate reasoning, combined with a simple, unaffected, and perspicuous style. At another bookstall I found his 'Treatise on Tar-water,' of which I read as much as I could. Full as it is of learning, I wondered at that time, as I wonder still, that the author of the ' Principles of Human Knowledge' and the 'Essay on Vision' should have produced another work with so many strange conceits and illogical conclusions as the ' *Tar-water.*' Berkeley's metaphysical head seems to have been totally unfitted for mere physical researches.

On the whole, the beginning of my London life was agreeable enough, though it formed a strange contrast to the quiet of my father's house. In the spring of 1802 I returned to Winterslow. I had never been absent before for more than a fortnight at a time, and once only even for so long a period as this. I began at last to suffer from a kind of nostalgia, and I shall never forget the delight which I felt when, seated in the little Salisbury coach, which performed its journey of eighty-two miles in about thirteen hours, I once more breathed the country air, and looked out on green fields and trees, or recognised the scenes of my boyhood gradually disclose themselves as I walked from the Winterslow Hut (two miles off) to my father's house. During the following summer (1802) I passed my time much as I had done formerly. I thought, however, that I ought to do something towards advancing my professional knowledge, and, accordingly, I borrowed Benjamin Bell's 'System of Surgery' from Mr. Wyche, one of the surgeons to the Salisbury Infirmary. I found it, however, a most unreadable production; indeed, I doubt whether it was ever read by any one. Yet, somehow, it had a sort of reputation in its day, which, I imagine, is to be attributed to its being the work of a leading surgeon in Edinburgh, and to its consisting of some half-dozen thick octavo volumes.

In the autumn I returned to London, and to our former residence near the Inns of Court. My elder brother, who had been staying in London during the summer, was a favourite pupil of Mr. Charles Butler, the eminent conveyancer, and the author of several literary works. Mr. Butler's family were at this time on the Continent (during a part of the short peace), and my brother having been ill, Mr. Butler very good-naturedly insisted on his staying with him at his house in Great Ormond Street. This introduced me to his acquaintance. He took, somehow, a liking to me, and from that time to the day of his death treated me with the greatest kindness. During the following winter I attended Mr. Wilson's lectures in Great Windmill Street, and worked hard in his dissecting-room. For learning anatomy, Mr. Wilson's school afforded much better opportunities than that of my former teacher. He had a most profound knowledge of his subject, and his demonstrations were very far superior to those of any other anatomist of that day; and I may, I believe, add, to those of any one since. He kept up the attention of the diligent students, who were really anxious to learn, not by the aid of happy illustrations and appropriate anecdotes, but by the quantity of instruction which he conveyed. For those of an inferior class, his lectures were almost too good. With them, a neighbouring teacher, who was more of a private tutor than an anatomist (*nomine* Carpue), was more popular.

During this my second, as well as my first, winter in London, my professional studies were wholly limited to anatomy, except that in the early part of it, and afterwards, when I had no subject for dissection, by Dr. Baillie's advice, I attended in a chemist's shop, in order that I might gain some knowledge of the Materia Medica, and the making up of prescriptions. The shop was at the corner of Little Newport Street, and the proprietor of it was Mr. Clifton, who also practised as an apothecary, exercising his

art among the tradesmen of the neighbourhood.
He was an apothecary of the old school, having
no science in the ordinary sense of the word;
yet, I have no doubt, a useful and successful
practitioner. I come to this conclusion because,
although there was nothing prepossessing in
either his manner or appearance, his practice
gradually increased, until at last he was able
to give up his shop and live in a large house
near Leicester Square, where he dispensed me-
dicines only to his own patients.   It is usual in
these days to regard this class of practitioners
with little respect; but the fact is, that they
were very useful persons, and, having no very
ambitious aspirations, they were within the
reach of the poorer orders of society, which is
not much the case with the better educated sur-
geon-apothecaries, or, as they are called, general
practitioners, of the present day, who have expended a considerable sum of money in order
to obtain a license to practise.   Mr. Clifton's
treatment of disease seemed to be very simple.
He had in his shop five large bottles, which were
labelled *Mistura Salina, Mistura Cathartica,*

Mistura Astringens, Mistura Cinchonæ, and another, of which I forget the name, but it was some kind of white emulsion for coughs; and it seemed to me that out of these five bottles he prescribed for two-thirds of his patients. I do not, however, set this down to his discredit; for I have observed that, while young members of the medical profession generally deal in a great variety of remedies, they generally discard the greater number of them as they grow older, until at last their treatment of diseases becomes almost as simple as that of the Æsculapius of Little Newport Street. There are some, indeed, who form an exception to this general rule, who, even to the last, seem to think that they have, or ought to have, a specific for everything, and are always making experiments with new remedies. The consequence is that they do not cure the patients, which the patients at last find out, and then they have no patients left.

During my attendance at the Windmill Street school I worked hard in the dissecting-room, and learned a good deal of anatomy. If I did so, however, it must be owned that it was rather as a duty, and because it was necessary to my future undertakings, than because I had any particular taste for the details of anatomical study. I remember some years afterwards dining with a friend (Henry Drummond, the present member of Parliament for West Surrey), who was a craniologist, at the Athenæum, when he told me that he saw that I had the organ of constructiveness much developed, and that this explained how it was that I excelled in the use of my hands, and was an excellent dissector. There was never a greater mistake. I was naturally very clumsy in the use of my hands, and it was only by taking great pains with myself that I became at all otherwise.

During this my second winter in London, I made only one acquaintance with whom I was at all intimate among my fellow-students, in the person of Mr. Rose, who ultimately became a surgeon of the same hospital with myself, and is still well known by a very valuable paper published in the 'Medico-Chirurgical Transactions.' Rose was a nephew of Dr. Reid, the author of the ' Inquiry into the Human Mind on the Principles of Common Sense,' and had been educated by him at Glasgow. From thence he was transplanted to Oxford as one of the Glasgow exhibitioners at Balliol, and then to London as a student in surgery. We lived very much together, and our friendship continued without a day's interruption until his death, about twenty-five years afterwards. He was a thoroughly honourable, high-minded man, having little imagination, but a very clear head and sound judgment. I have no doubt that my intimacy with him tended very much to the improvement of my own character, and I look back to the friendship which existed between us as one of the most happy circumstances of my life. This excellent man belonged to a family who had a tendency to pulmonary disease. In the year 1828 he had the misfortune to lose three out of four children from the effects of scarlet fever. This broke his heart. The disease of which his brothers and sisters had been the victims became developed in himself, and he soon followed his children to the grave.

In the spring of 1803 I first entered as a pupil

under Mr. (afterwards Sir Everard) Home, at St. George's Hospital.

At this time Mr. Home was the leading surgeon at the west end of London. He was looked up to with something like veneration by all the hospital pupils. He was punctual in his attendance, performed his duties with great ability, and was far above all his colleagues, both in his diagnosis of disease and as an operating surgeon. As a practical surgeon, I do not think that Mr. Thomas Keate, the senior surgeon, was at all his inferior; indeed, the latter had rather an advantage over him in the medical treatment of his patients. But Mr. Keate occupied what at that time was a very high station as surgeon-general to the army. In the time of war this was a place of great responsibility, with the disadvantage, for so it is, of a very extensive patronage. Partly in consequence of his time being thus very much occupied, and partly from being naturally of unpunctual habits, he was negligent of his hospital duties, and he was not estimated as, with his talents and knowledge, he would have been otherwise.

I had now left my old lodgings, where I lived with my brother Peter, in Carey Street, and resided in the neighbourhood of the hospital, in order that I might be better able to attend to my hospital studies. At this period I made one valuable addition to my professional acquaintance, Nicolson, who is still living, though in dilapidated health, at Calcutta. He was some years older than myself, was a *protégé* of Mr. Home, had a house opposite his in Sackville Street, and assisted him in his private practice. He was a man of considerable talents, and an excellent practical surgeon, but with no taste for the science of his profession. Three years afterwards he went to India in the service of the East India Company, where, from the high character which he brought with him, he had at once an office given him which enabled him to reside at the seat of government. He soon obtained a very large and lucrative private practice in Calcutta, besides acquiring a great degree of popularity, to which his kind disposition and open and manly character justly entitled him.

The commencement of my studies at the hospital was that of a completely new era in my life. Hitherto it is true that I had worked hard enough. With the exception of Lawrence, I doubt whether any one of my acquaintance had been equally diligent. But it was rather as a matter of duty, or I rather ought to say of necessity, than because I felt any very great interest in what I was doing; and most willingly, if I could have afforded it, would I have turned my back on anatomy and returned to literary pursuits. A great change took place as soon as I became familiar with the business of the hospital.

To those who really desire to learn, the wards of a hospital are soon found to be replete with interest. At first all is confusion. The nice distinction of symptoms on which the diagnosis of disease depends, why the pulse in one case indicates immediate danger, and in another none at all, why one patient recovers and another dies, why the same kind of treatment is successful in one instance and fails in another,—these, and a multitude of other matters, are quite inexplicable to the young student. Everything is seen as it were through a mist. After no long time, however, the mist begins to clear away, and whoever has advanced thus far finds no difficulty afterwards. Every case is an interesting subject of enquiry. A great game is being played, in which the stake is often neither more nor less than the life or death of a fellow-creature, and in which those among the students who devote themselves to their business perform a humble yet not unimportant part without any painful feeling of responsibility. Not many months elapsed before I became sensible of the good effect of these new studies, and of the wisdom of Dr. Baillie's advice that I should make myself a tolerably complete anatomist before I commenced my attendance at the hospital; as I found that I was able to comprehend many things that were passing under my observation which I could never have properly comprehended otherwise, and in which those who were less prepared in this respect were little able to understand.

During the summer of 1803 I never failed to pass the early part of the day in the wards of the hospital. In the afternoon I usually dined by myself at my lodgings in Knightsbridge, and in the evening read some Latin classics, and other books which formed my scanty library, or a novel from a small circulating library at Brompton, or walked in Kensington Gardens. As the season advanced, most of my friends left London. A few, however, remained, whom I met occasionally; among them was Dibdin, since known by his works on Bibliography, who at that time resided at Kensington, not very far from my lodgings at Knightsbridge, and with whom I occasionally wandered to hear the nightingales in the lane beyond Holland House. In September I returned to my father's house at Winterslow, intending to remain there only for a short time, and to be in London again when the lectures in Windmill Street were resumed on the 1st of October. I had not, however, been long in the country before I had an attack of fever, which confined me for some time to my bed. On my recovery, my father took me to the seaside at Mudeford, in Hampshire, from whence I returned to London at the end of October. This was the last opportunity I had of seeing my father. He drove me in his phaeton to Lymington, where I found the mail-coach which conveyed me to Southampton. On the following morning I embarked in one of the long stage-coaches then in use (like a modern omnibus), which conveyed me to London. It was a melancholy journey. My father's health was visibly failing; though, as far as my bodily powers were concerned, I had pretty well recovered from the effects of my illness, my animal spirits were at a very low ebb. I had never before, and have never since then, been in so desponding a state of mind; and I shall never forget the feelings which oppressed me as I passed through the romantic scenery of the New Forest, or as I sate on the following day, with eleven other passengers, in the slow-going long coach. It seemed as if I was not equal to climbing the mountain which lay before me; yet I was sensible that I had no alternative, and that I must either climb it or starve. This state of mind, however, was not of long duration: I was soon hard at work, and forgot my anxieties.

I now removed to some lodgings in May Fair, which, being situated between Hyde Park Corner and Great Windmill Street, enabled me more easily to divide my studies between the hospital and the school of anatomy. At the latter I had obtained some credit with Mr. Wilson and his colleague Mr. Thomas. The latter only delivered a few of the anatomical lectures, but it was understood that he was to superintend the dissections, and give an anatomical demonstration for an hour daily in the dissecting-room. He was not very fond of his vocation as a teacher, and as he was acquiring a considerable share of private practice, he was led to play truant a good deal. When he did so, he was accustomed to ask me to give the demonstration in his place; an arrangement which was attended with no difficulty, as both Mr. Wilson and the students were, or seemed to be, well satisfied with it, and as I felt myself sufficiently rewarded for the trouble which it gave me by the position in which it placed me above that of the ordinary students.

During this winter (1803–1804) I still con-

tinued to attend the meetings of the Academical
Society, and kept up my intercourse with my
former friends about the Inns of Court. By
great prudence I continued to live with sufficient
comfort without making more than a very moderate demand on my father's limited means, and
was never once in debt. I felt, however, that it
would be very convenient to me indeed to have
a little more money at my disposal. Some of
my friends at this time obtained some additions
to their incomes by writing for magazines and
other publications. Ellis especially in great
measure maintained himself in that way, and it
came into my mind that I might follow his example. I offered a disquisition on the study of
metaphysics to Richard Phillips, who published
the 'Monthly Magazine' (and who was afterwards Sir Richard Phillips, and himself the
author of a crazy work on Natural Philosophy).
Phillips declined to accept it, in which he was
quite right; it was a very absurd production.
He did not, however, altogether decline my services. One of his speculations was the publication of a book under the name of 'The Annual

Biography,' and, knowing that I had lived in
Wiltshire, he proposed that I should write the
life of Beckford of Fonthill, the author of 'Va-
thek.' As I knew nothing of this individual
except some general reports, of which the less
was said the better, I declined the proposal. I
then offered some papers on literary subjects to
Baldwin's 'Literary Journal,' a magazine which
has been long since extinct. These were trum-
pery enough; nevertheless they were favourably
received, and my vanity was soon gratified by
seeing myself for the first time in print. The
editor wrote to me that he was in my debt, and
that I might receive a small sum that was owing
to me whenever I could go to New Bridge Street
for the purpose. I know not how it was that
I never applied for the money. I found that I
could not well follow two trades at the same
time, and thus my literary adventures soon came
to an end.

I have mentioned that when I parted with my
father in the previous autumn his health was a
good deal failing. It continued to fail through
the winter, but he was so anxious not to inter-

fere with the studies of my elder brother and
myself that he would not allow us to be informed
of it.   In March an alteration for the worse took
place rather suddenly ; and before we were aware
that his life was in any real danger he was no
more.   I had never before known what it was
to lose any one for whom I had much affection,
and I felt the loss most acutely.   It dwelt on
my mind long afterwards, and I well remember
that for some months he was continually present
to me in my dreams.   My uncle, Charles Collins, who was an unmarried man, invited our
whole family to his house at Salisbury, where
we remained until after the funeral.   I then returned to London forlorn enough, but less so
than I should have been if I had not found
much kindness and sympathy among some of
my relations, especially Dr. and Mrs. Denman,
Lady Staunton, and my cousins Mrs. Baillie
and the present Sir George Staunton.   The latter was two years older than myself, had been
my playfellow when we were boys, and has continued my intimate friend, without our friendship having been interrupted for one instant,

even to the present day. He was at this time a writer in the East India Company's factory at Canton, but was in England on leave of absence, and living with his mother.

I must avail myself of this last opportunity of saying a few words more respecting my father. I have already expressed how great our obligations are to him for the pains which he took with the education of my brothers and myself. It is still a matter of surprise with me that he should by himself have been able to do so much for us in the way of instruction as he did. But I owe him much more for the example which he set us as a man of the most strict integrity and honour, with an almost chivalrous notion of independence. He taught us to trust to nothing but our own character and conduct; and to disdain the attaining advantages by any other means. In early life, having lived much with Lord Holland and his friends, he had been what was then called a *Foxite*, and he continued to be a Liberal in politics to the last. This, in a worldly point of view, was much to his disadvantage, as, for many years before he died, a violent party spirit prevailed, and the Tory party were predominant. He was a Liberal in other matters also, having no kind of horror of Dissenters. He was a sincerely religious person, but he made no parade of his religion. He made us read Butler's 'Analogy' and Paley's 'Evidences,' but never discussed such abstruse points in theology as those which agitate men's minds in the present contentious age. His great fault, and indeed the only one of which I have any recollection, was a hasty and impetuous temper; but this was combined with great tenderness and kindness of disposition. If he was sometimes wanting in that degree of patience which is essential in a tutor having to deal with his pupils whose wits are not equally bright on all occasions, his affection for us was unvarying. He was always anxious to promote our innocent recreations, and I have no doubt that the great object of his ambition was to qualify us to become happy and useful members of society in after life.

Some time after the loss of my father, my mother removed from Winterslow to a house in

the immediate neighbourhood of Salisbury. The
situation was convenient to her, as it brought
her near to my grandmother and my uncle
Charles Collins. Her income was very limited,
being reduced still further by an income-tax of
ten per cent.; and being, moreover, rendered
less efficient than it would have been at the
present day in consequence of the high prices,
not only of provisions, but of all other com-
modities. The dearness of things depended
partly on the great demand occasioned by the
expensive war in which the country was engaged, partly on increased taxation, partly on
the depreciation of bank-notes under Mr. Pitt's
Bank Restriction Act. The possessors of real
property were flourishing; the income of professional persons kept pace with the times; and
the proprietors of Bank of England stock shared
large profits at the expense of the community,
in the shape of frequent *bonuses*; but persons
of fixed incomes were sadly straitened, and my
mother was one of them. She was, however,
an excellent manager, prudent, careful, and as
free from selfishness as it is possible for any one

to be. She at once determined that she would do her best to maintain my brother and myself in the course on which we had entered, and partly out of her income, and partly by not hesitating to sink a portion of her capital, she was enabled to do so. Of course this could not have been accomplished, as far as my elder brother and myself were concerned, if we ourselves had not partaken of her care and prudence. By avoiding all extravagances we continued to live with as much comfort, and to keep up as respectable an appearance, as many of our associates whose means were larger than our own, and who indeed were not unfrequently in difficulties which we were able to avoid.

During the summer of 1804, a friend of mine, of the name of Jeffreys, was house surgeon of the hospital, and my intimacy with him enabled me to pursue my studies there with great advantage. He had more knowledge of his profession than most young men of his standing. In the early part of the day, I was always with him in the wards; and in the evening, we were generally together. It was from him that I

first learned the importance of keeping written
notes of cases, a practice which I continued
ever afterwards. These notes I have carefully
preserved. They now form many thick quarto
volumes of manuscripts, to which (and even to
the earliest of them) I not unfrequently refer
with advantage, even at this advanced period of
my professional life. My custom has been to
take short notes at the bedside of the patients
in the day, and to expand them with the aid of
my memory in the evening. Thus they became
an exercise of the memory, and, instead of
weakening, tended to strengthen that important
faculty. After an experience of nearly fifty
years, I am satisfied that no one can be well
acquainted with his profession, either as a physician or surgeon, who has not studied it in that
manner. It is only by these means that a case
can be thoroughly and scientifically investigated,
or that that minute and accurate knowledge
of it can be obtained which is necessary to a
right diagnosis. For one who is to occupy
hereafter the situation of a consulting practitioner, to whom younger or less experienced

persons will apply for assistance in cases of doubt or difficulty, it answers another purpose, as it enables him to express himself with greater facility, and especially to give written opinions with a degree of clearness and precision with which he could not give them otherwise. I have always, during the many years in which I was a teacher and a hospital surgeon, endeavoured to impress on the minds of my pupils the necessity of making and preserving such written records of their experience; and I have often been pained to observe how small a proportion have followed the advice which I gave them. Some of them find a difficulty in doing so from the want of original education, and really not having a sufficient knowledge of the use of language even for this simple kind of literary composition; others neglect it from mere idleness; while the great mass of students, whose period of professional education is limited, are so occupied by the great (and, as I think, unnecessary) number of lectures which they are now required to attend, and in running from one class-room to another, that they really have

neither the leisure nor the physical powers
necessary for pursuing, in any efficient manner,
the practical study of disease in the wards of
the hospital.

Although I had now become much interested
in my hospital studies, I passed a great part of
my time during the following winter (1804–
1805) in the Anatomical School, where, in consequence of Mr. Thomas having become still
more occupied with his private practice, I had
almost the exclusive superintendence of the dissecting-room, under Mr. Wilson, who generally
appeared there for a very short time in the forenoon. Mr. Home had made an arrangement
by which I was to become house surgeon of the
hospital in the following Midsummer, this being
then, as it now is, an office held during twelve
months by one of the better-informed students.
At the end of the anatomical session, however,
a circumstance occurred, the effect of which was
to disturb this arrangement. Mr. Thomas determined to retire from his office as a teacher of
anatomy, and Mr. Wilson proposed to me that I
should succeed him as the demonstrator in the
School. . . . .

[A portion of the MS. is wanting.]*

. . . . they agreed that I should supply his place, with the understanding that I should be at liberty to vacate the office in the latter part of the autumn, as soon as I found that my duty as a teacher of anatomy rendered it necessary for me to do so. This was a very fortunate circumstance, as my residence in the hospital, even for six months, enabled me to obtain a great deal of knowledge as to the details of surgical practice which it would have cost me a great deal of trouble to obtain otherwise.

I must not pass over this part of my life without noticing a very great advantage which I possessed during the period of my professional education, compared with what I should have had if I had lived in these later times. No

* The omission probably consisted of a paragraph stating that Mr. Jeffreys was about to vacate the office of house-surgeon, and that Sir B. Brodie was to be appointed in his place—which was the case. He held that office from May to November, 1805, when he resigned it to undertake the duties of teacher of anatomy in the Windmill Street School.— *Note from the complete edition of Sir B. Brodie's Works, edited by Mr. C. Hawkins.*

rules were then laid down as to the number of lectures which I was required to attend. The examination at the College of Surgeons was sufficiently good, as far as it went, but it was of a very simple and elementary kind. It was no more than a diligent student might pass without any special preparation for the purpose.

The consequence was, that I was enabled to take my education very much upon myself; and I soon found that I could nohow obtain so much useful knowledge as by a diligent attendance on the dissecting-room, and on the wards of the hospital. I cannot say that I neglected the use of books, but it was more in the way of reference and illustration than by a regular course of reading. I attended lectures on Anatomy, and, during one season, Dr. Crichton's lectures on the Practice of Physic, Materia Medica, and Chemistry, the latter especially with some advantage. During my first season in London, I had entered as a pupil to Mr. Abernethy's lectures on Surgery; but having at that time seen no surgical practice, I did not understand them, and soon ceased to attend them. I afterwards

entered to some other lectures on Surgery, at
the West-end of the town, but found that I
learned nothing from them, so I ceased to attend
there also. Mr. Home was accustomed to give
an annual course of twelve surgical lectures
gratuitously to the pupils of the hospital. These
were excellent, and I attended them, year after
year, with great advantage. Altogether, I do
not suppose that I attended one-fourth of the
number of lectures which the unfortunate students are now required to listen to under the
direction of the constituted authorities. But
I was acquiring knowledge in other ways, and
much more substantial knowledge than can be
acquired from such dull and humdrum discourses
as lectures usually are; and, which is better
still, I had leisure to make my own observations,
to think and reflect. Nor was this style of
education peculiar to myself. I remember when
Mr. Abernethy complained that Lawrence would
not attend lectures. My friends and contemporaries, Jeffreys and Lawrence, took the same
course; and so it had been with Nicolson, who
was some few years in advance of us. I can

easily conceive that, if I had been compelled to sit on the benches of a theatre four or five hours daily, or tempted to compete for prizes as students are, and to get crammed for various examinations, my position in life afterwards would have been very different from what it has been in reality.

It so happened that when I was about to give up my office as house surgeon to the hospital, Nicolson, whom I have just mentioned, being engaged to be married, and finding that some few years might probably elapse before he could conveniently do so if he waited for practice in London, determined to seek his fortune elsewhere, and accepted an appointment in the service of the East India Company in Bengal ; and that Mr. Home proposed to me that I should supply his place by assisting him in his private operations. I conclude that he thought that I should answer his purpose in this respect, but I know that he was partly led to do so by the circumstance of my having made myself a pretty good anatomist, and by the wish to have my help in carrying out the enquiries in comparative anatomy in which he was generally engaged. As these occupations were quite compatible with those which I had in the Windmill Street School, I was very glad to undertake them. They afforded me the means of learning much as to my profession which cannot be well learned in a hospital; and further, by initiating me in the study of anatomy and physiology generally, without limiting my views merely to that which is required for surgical practice, they led me to scientific enquiries, which for many years afterwards formed a most agreeable addition to the drudgery of my every-day duties. My connection with Mr. Home also made some addition to my income, as I saw those of his patients who were disposed to have the advice of so young a man as I was while he was in the country for three weeks in September, and as I also received a few fees on some other occasions. My gains, however, in this way were very small; Mr. Home never had a very large practice, such as at all corresponded to his reputation. One year, and that was before I knew him, he had received about 6,700*l.* in fees. This was much less than

what Mr. Cline, or Sir Astley Cooper, or myself, have received since; but his income while I
knew him never, I imagine, amounted to 5,000*l.*,
and as he had a large family and lived expen-
sively, he had nothing to spare out of it for
others.   Still, what I gained from that source
and from teaching anatomy, enabled me to make
a somewhat smaller demand on my mother's
slender means; and as I always looked to the
future, and not to the present results of my
exertions, I was quite contented.

For nearly two years and a half after I had
ceased to reside at the hospital as house surgeon,
there was little change in my pursuits or mode
of life.   During the greater part of that time
I lived in lodgings in Sackville Street.   The
winter months supplied me with a good deal of
occupation in the dissecting-room; and whatever time I could spare from my duties as a
teacher of anatomy was well devoted to the hospital.   I assisted Mr. Home in his private operations and on some other occasions, and to a still
greater extent in his researches in comparative
anatomy.   In this latter employment I was

associated a good deal with Mr. Clift, the conservator of the museum of the College of Surgeons. I ought not to mention Mr. Clift's name
without expressing not only how much I am
indebted to him for the information which he
afforded me on the subjects with which he was
conversant, but also the great esteem which I
have always had for his general character. His
history, as I have heard it related by those who
were acquainted with it, was nearly as follows:
—Mr. Hunter was acquainted with Mrs. Gilbert,
a lady of fortune in Cornwall. In conversation
with her he observed that he had great difficulty
in obtaining fit persons to assist him in making
his anatomical museum, and that he believed that
his best way would be himself to educate a lad
especially for this purpose. Mrs. Gilbert said
that she knew a very clever boy, who was accustomed to come into her kitchen in Cornwall and
make drawings with chalk on the floor, who
would, with proper instruction, become an excellent draughtsman, and who, from the ability
which he displayed, would probably answer his
purpose very well in other matters; and she

F

offered to negotiate with the boy and his parents
or him to come to London on trial. Mr. Hunter
gladly availed himself of this offer, and the nego-
tiation ended in Clift becoming an inmate in
Hunter's house. I do not know the exact date,
but I believe that this was not more than two
or three years before Hunter's death. On the
occurrence of this event, Hunter's executors
(Dr. Baillie and Mr. Home) engaged Clift to
take charge of the museum until they had found
the means of disposing of it for the benefit of
his family; and when it was purchased by Parliament, and consigned to the care of the College
of Surgeons, the council of the college retained
him for the same purpose, under the name of
conservator, a situation which he retained during
the remainder of his life.

Clift's early education had probably not extended beyond reading and writing, but he had
a vast desire of acquiring knowledge; had read
a great deal in an irregular manner; but his
chief study was that of the museum in which he
lived for many years; and with this he had a
more intimate acquaintance than any other per-

son after the death of the great philosopher by whom it was founded. He had great sagacity, great powers of observation, and great memory, but he wanted that method which a better early education would have afforded him; and his knowledge, though extensive, was of a very desultory kind. His devotion to the memory of Hunter, and his attachment to the museum, formed a remarkable feature of his character, at the same time that his simplicity of mind, his disinterestedness, and the kindness of his disposition, gained him the affection of all who knew him.

It was during the period of which I am now speaking, and not very long after I had ceased to be house surgeon, that Mr. Home introduced me to Sir Joseph Banks. Sir Joseph took much interest in any one who was in any way engaged in the pursuit of science, and as I suppose, partly from Home's recommendation, and partly from knowing that I was occupied with him in making dissections in comparative anatomy, was led to show me much kindness and attention, such as it was very agreeable for

so young a man to receive from so distinguished
a person.   He invited me to the meetings which
were held in his library on the Sunday evenings
which intervened between the meetings of the .
Royal Society.   These meetings were of a very
different kind from those larger assemblies which
were held three or four times in the season by
the Duke of Sussex, the Marquis of Northamp-
ton, and Lord Rosse, and they were much more
useful.   There was no crowding together of
noblemen and philosophers and would-be philosophers, nor any kind of magnificent display.
The visitors consisted of those who were already
distinguished by their scientific reputation, of
some younger men who, like myself, were following these greater persons at a humble dis-
tance, of a few individuals of high station who,
though not working men themselves, were regarded by Sir Joseph as patrons of science,
of such foreigners of distinction as during the
war were to be found in London, and of very
few besides.   Everything was conducted in the
plainest manner.   Tea was handed round to the
company, and there were no other refreshments.

But here were to be seen the elder Herschel, Davy, Wollaston, Young, Hatchett, Wilkins the Sanscrit scholar, Marsden, Major Rennell, Henry Cavendish, Home, Barrow, Maskelyne, Blagden, Abernethy, Carlisle, and others who have long since passed away, but whose reputation still remains, and gives a character to the age in which they lived.

In the course of the first few years which elapsed after my introduction to Sir Joseph Banks, I derived so much advantage from the society which I met in his library, and occasionally at his dinner-table, that I feel it in some measure a duty not to omit some further notice of this eminent individual. I have been informed by those who might be supposed to be well acquainted with his history, that as a boy at Eton he was a very indifferent student of Greek and Latin, and that he was himself mortified to find how much less a proficient he was in the school exercises than his fellow-pupils. But even at this early period he began the study of plants; examining the different parts of their structure, and laying the foundation of that extensive

knowledge for which he was afterwards distinguished in this department of natural history.
Having inherited a considerable fortune, he had
no taste for the usual trifling pursuits of affluent
young men, and being of an enterprising disposition, he obtained permission to accompany
Captain Cook in one (I believe the first) of his
voyages of discovery in the Pacific Ocean.   I
do not know how soon it was after his return to
England that he was elected President of the
Royal Society, superseding the former President,
Sir John Pringle.   His election took place after
a severe contest, in which his principal opponents
were the mathematicians, with Dr. Horsley, the
Bishop of Rochester, at their head.   He was
created a Baronet, a Civil Knight of the Bath
(corresponding to the G.C.B. of the present
time), and a Privy Councillor.   He was annually
re-elected to the presidential chair for many
years, resigning the office as soon as he found
that his declining health prevented his attending
the meetings, that being not long before he died.

His London residence was in Soho Square,
there being extensive premises behind his dwell-

ing-house, which contained his library and his botanical collection. The former consisted chiefly of books on Natural History and the transactions of learned societies, and was probably in these departments unrivalled in the world. His principal librarian was a Swede, Dr. Dryander; and under his superintendence the library was so well managed that, although books were lent to men of science in the most liberal manner, I believe that not a volume was ever lost. Dryander was indeed a pattern as a librarian. The library over which he presided was to him *all in all*. Without being a man of science himself, he knew every book, and the contents of every book in it. If any one enquired of him where he might look for information on any particular subject, he would go first to one shelf, then to another, and return with a bundle of books under his arm containing the information which was desired.

Besides Dryander, there were two others who acted as sub-librarians, and Dr. Brown, the botanist, who had the charge of the botanical collection. Brown had formerly been engaged as naturalist in Captain Flinder's expedition of discovery. At the time of which I am speaking, he might be seen daily in Sir Joseph's library, dissecting plants, and accumulating those stores of knowledge which have since gained for him the reputation of being the first botanist and botanical physiologist in the world, and the honour of being one of the very limited number of foreign associates of the Academy of Sciences of Paris. By his will, Sir Joseph directed that Brown should receive an annuity during his life, on condition of his taking charge of his library, which was still to be accessible to men of science as heretofore. He further directed that after Brown's death the library should be transferred to the British Museum. It being, however, found that a more convenient arrangement might be made both for Brown and for the public, the trustees of the Museum appointed Brown keeper of the botany in that institution, and the library was at once transferred to its ultimate destination.

The attention which Sir Joseph Banks paid to the affairs of the Royal Society was unremitting. He was very much of an autocrat, but, like other successful autocrats, he maintained his authority by consulting the feelings and opinions of others, and no one complained of it. There is no doubt that his ample fortune, and his devotion of it to purposes of natural science, made his task more easy than it would have been otherwise; still, he could not have accomplished what he did if he had not possessed a great knowledge of human nature. It was by a combination of these means that he was enabled to exercise his influence over the philosophers, so that every one among them looked up to him as a friend and counsellor; and that he succeeded in keeping in abeyance among them those feelings of jealousy from which even those who, standing apart from mere vulgar pursuits, devote themselves to the acquisition of knowledge, are not altogether exempt.

During the greater part of the summer, Sir Joseph resided at his house in Lincolnshire, where he occupied himself chiefly with agricultural pursuits, and in presiding over agricultural meetings. In November he returned to

his house in Soho Square, in time to be present at the first meeting of the Royal Society.
During the winter, besides the weekly evening
meetings in his library, he was in the habit of
entertaining parties of scientific men at dinner.
Every morning he had a sort of public breakfast
in his library, at which foreigners of distinction
and others were introduced to him. As the
spring advanced he left his house in London to
reside at a villa known as ' Spring Grove,' near
Hounslow, where he remained until the session
of the Royal Society terminated. Here he dined
daily at four o'clock, in order that his frequent
visitors from London might have ample time to
return home in the evening. When the weather
permitted, his guests adjourned to have tea and
coffee under the cedars in the garden. In the
intermediate time it was not unusual to visit
his hot-houses and conservatories, under the
auspices of his unmarried sister, Miss Banks;
or the dairy, which was under the especial care
of Lady Banks, who was proud of displaying a
magnificent collection of old china-ware which
was there deposited. These parties at Spring

Grove were not the less agreeable because they generally consisted of few persons, and everything was conducted in a simple and unostentatious manner.

On the whole, it is difficult to conceive that any one could perform his duties as President of the Royal Society in a manner more honourable to himself, or more beneficial to the community, than that in which they were performed by Sir Joseph Banks. It is to be observed at the same time that he had some peculiar advantages, having an ample fortune and no family, and having also the good taste to avoid being involved in political discussions and disputes.

In March, 1808, through the interest of Mr. Home, with the assistance of his colleague, and of some little reputation which I had myself acquired as a young teacher of anatomy, I was elected assistant-surgeon to St. George's Hospital. I was fortunate in obtaining such an appointment so early in life. I was indeed not quite twenty-five years of age (my birthday being in June). I was at that time living in lodgings at No. 24 Sackville Street, not having my name on the door as a candidate for private practice, and being still one of the senior students at the hospital. From the date of my appointment Mr. Home left me very much of the management of his patients, and by degrees interfered in it very little himself. This, however, was not the only advantage which I derived from my new office. The junior surgeon, Mr. Gunning, joined Lord Wellington's army in the Peninsula, being attached to the staff of the commander-in-chief as surgeon-in-chief of the British forces. There was an old law of the hospital (now abrogated) which enabled the Weekly Board to give an unlimited leave of absence to any one of the medical officers who was employed on military service. This leave was granted to Mr. Gunning. The governors at the same time appointed the other assistant-surgeon, Mr. Robert Keate, and myself to take charge of his patients in his absence. This arrangement continued until the year 1813, when, on the resignation of Mr. Thomas Keate, his nephew was elected surgeon in his place; and from that time until Mr. Gunning resumed his duties, about four years afterwards, his patients were entirely under my management. Thus I had the opportunity, at an unusually early age, of acquiring a large experience in hospital practice, and to this circumstance my early professional success may very much be attributed. Having at this time no private practice, I was able to devote a great deal of my time to my duties in the hospital. During six months in the year I passed several hours daily in the wards, taking notes of cases, and communicating freely with the students. During the other six months, the whole of the time which I could spare from my employment as a teacher of anatomy, was devoted to the hospital also. The custom at St. George's, and indeed at all the other metropolitan hospitals, had hitherto been for the surgeons to go round the wards only on two days in the week, not attending otherwise, except when there were operations to perform, or severe accidents which made their assistance necessary, or on other special occasions. Mr. Robert Keate and myself

were the first persons who adopted another mode
of proceeding. We were at our posts in the
hospital daily, and superintended everything;
and there was never an urgent case which we
did not visit in the evening, and not unfrequently at an early hour in the morning also.
This was of as much advantage to the students
as it was to the patients and ourselves, and the
effect of it was soon perceptible, in the increase
of zeal and diligence on their part, and in their
increasing numbers. After some time I appointed clinical clerks, one for the patients of
Mr. Home (or, as he became soon afterwards,
Sir Everard Home) and another for those who
were under my care as officiating for Mr. Gunning. I also began to deliver clinical lectures;
and I believe that these were the first lectures
of this kind which were ever delivered in a
London hospital.

I may take this opportunity of saying a few
words respecting my friend and colleague Mr.
Robert Keate. At the time of which I am
speaking, his uncle held the very high and important office of surgeon-general to the army,

and he himself was a deputy-inspector of military hospitals, and assisted his uncle in his official duties.   He had been introduced by his uncle to the Royal Family, with whom he was a considerable favourite; was surgeon to the Queen, and to some of the royal dukes and princesses.   These various avocations for a considerable time had interfered with his devoting himself so much to the business of the hospital as he would have done otherwise; nevertheless he had already obtained a very considerable practical knowledge of his profession, and was an excellent operator.   We acted together as colleagues until I resigned my office as surgeon in the year 1840; and it is, I hope, to the credit of both of us that, during the whole of those thirty-two years, the most perfect harmony and friendship always subsisted between us.   We had the most implicit confidence in each other; and not only did we never openly disagree, but I do not believe that either of us entertained even unkind thoughts as to the other.   He was, and still is, a perfect gentleman in every sense of the word; kind in his feelings; open, honest, and upright in his conduct. His professional knowledge and his general character made him a most useful officer of the hospital : and, now that our *game has been played*, it is with great satisfaction that I look back to the long and disinterested friendship that existed between us.

For a year or two before I was elected assistant-surgeon at the hospital, Mr. Wilson had been anxious that I should join with him in delivering lectures on surgery, in the theatre in Great Windmill Street, in addition to those delivered by him on anatomy. I had, however, declined to do so, not feeling that either from my knowledge or my position I was equal to the task. On my becoming connected with the hospital, however, the case was altered. I could now refer to my own experience and my own practice, and I had a place in my profession which I had not previously. The consequence was that in the October of 1808, Mr. Wilson and myself began a course of surgical lectures. Mr. Wilson delivered in each course about a dozen lectures, the remainder, and of course the much greater number, being delivered by myself. After the second year Mr. Wilson retired from the surgical lectures altogether, and from that time the whole of these lectures were given by myself, until I resigned them to Mr. Babington and Mr. Hawkins nearly twenty years afterwards. My lectures were very well attended, not only by the students of our own Anatomical School, but also by those of Mr. Brookes's Anatomical School in Blenheim Street. My stock of knowledge at first must necessarily have been very limited, and for many years my delivery was constrained and awkward. Nevertheless my lectures were very popular. The explanation of this I apprehend to be that whatever information I gave was drawn from or confirmed by my own observation, and not taken from books, and that I was really in earnest in my endeavours to instruct my pupils. I took great pains in the composition of my lectures, referring to and analysing my manuscript notes of cases, and comparing the results at which I had arrived with those recorded by the last surgical writers. At first I wrote about half-a-dozen lectures at full length. But I soon found that it was

G

needless, and almost impossible, to pursue this plan as to the entire course, and I therefore contented myself with making pretty full notes, and then abridging them to take with me into the theatre.

Soon after I had begun to deliver surgical lectures, Mr. Wilson, who had now obtained a considerable share of private practice, proposed that I should give a part of each anatomical course also.   This necessarily imposed on me a considerable addition to my labours.   At nine or ten o'clock in the evening, after my day's work was concluded, I had to arrange my lectures for the following day, and this frequently occupied me until three or four o'clock on the following morning.   On the days on which I had no evening lecture, having a pretty large acquaintance, I was very much engaged in dinner society, which, however, I never allowed to interfere with my more serious occupation, being of temperate habits, and always returning home at an early hour.

Besides my business at the hospital, the composition and delivery of my lectures, and the su-

perintendence of the dissecting-room, I assisted
Mr. Home in his operations in private practice,
visited some of his patients when unforeseen
circumstances occurred, and he was out of the
way, and made some dissections with him and
Mr. Clift in comparative anatomy. Thus, although I had nothing that deserved the name
of private practice, my life was one of great
occupation. I had, however, although not of a
robust constitution, considerable powers of en-
during fatigue. My health was sufficiently good,
and my prospects of advancement in my profession were as good as possible; and I have no
doubt that the cheerful spirits which these gave
me enabled me to accomplish easily what it
would have been difficult for me to accomplish
otherwise.

It was somewhere about this time that Dr.
Bateman proposed to me to join Dr. Henderson
and himself in the publication of a periodical
medical work, under the title of the 'Medical
Annual Register,' which was to consist partly
of reviews of medical books, partly of miscel-
laneous intelligence connected with the medical

sciences. I declined taking any active part in the management of it, but promised to contribute some articles, at the same time suggesting that they should apply to Lawrence for his assistance also. The work was not very popular, and, after the appearance of a second volume, died a natural death. My own contributions were only to the first volume, and if my recollection be accurate, were only three in number; namely, a review of Dr. Hooper's 'Anatomist's *Vade Mecum*,' of Cooper's 'Surgical Dictionary,' and another of ' A Treatise on Lithotomy,' by an Edinburgh surgeon of the name of Allan. The truth is that, with the exception of Dr. Bateman, who was older and more experienced than the rest of us, there was no one among us who had sufficient practical knowledge to be qualified to do justice to such an undertaking, and I have looked back at it ever since as a very foolish concern, in which it would have been much wiser for me never to have interfered. I need scarcely add that I have never repeated the mistake, or written another medical review, unless an article on homœopathy and other quackeries, published in the ' Quarterly Review ' for December 1842, deserves that appellation.

Hitherto I had lived in lodgings at No. 24, in Sackville Street, with very indifferent accommodation, for which, however, I paid 100*l.* per annum; but in the autumn of 1809 I took a house at 22 in the same street, my mother having advanced me the money required for the purchase of the lease, and furnishing it. Now, for the first time, I placed my name on the door, and began to think seriously of private practice. I was able to accommodate three private pupils in my new residence, and this made an addition to my income sufficient to make up the difference between my expenses as a lodger and as a housekeeper. In the following year, in addition to a somewhat increasing income from my surgical lectures, I obtained between 200*l.* and 300*l.* from my private practice. Thus, in one way or another, I became much at ease as to my pecuniary circumstances, without having occasion to make any further demands on my mother. I was never once in debt, had always some money in hand, and being thus free from any great anxiety, I was able, in the spring of 1810, to engage with some considerable interest in some physiological enquiries on my own account, having been led to do so chiefly by the perusal of those very remarkable books, for which we are indebted to the genius of Bichat. I had previously communicated a paper to the Royal Society, which I now hold to be of little, or rather of no value. The council, however, thought it worthy of being printed in the 'Philosophical Transactions.' On the strength of it, Sir Joseph Banks agreed that I should be proposed a Fellow of the Royal Society, and my election took place without opposition. During the winter of 1810 and 1811 I communicated to the Society two physiological papers; one, 'On the Influence of the Brain on the Action of the Heart, and the Generation of Animal Heat,' and the other, 'On the Effects produced by certain Vegetable Poisons.' The former of these was given as the Croonian Lecture in November, 1810. They made a favourable impression at the time, so much so, that the Council awarded me the Copley medal in the autumn of 1811.   At this time I was only twenty-eight years of age.   I was told that when the question as to my having the medal was discussed in the Council, the only objection made to it was by one of the Councillors, who observed that it had never before been given to so young a man; on which Dr. Wollaston observed, that he thought if I deserved the medal, that was only an additional reason for my having it.   Few events that have occurred to me have gratified me so much as this.   This was, on the whole, a very happy period of my life.   The most distinguished Fellows of the Royal Society whom I was accustomed frequently to meet at Sir Joseph Banks's and elsewhere, treated me with much consideration and kindness, and I obtained a place in my profession which I could not have obtained otherwise.   Of course, I was not exempt from those anxieties to which all who depend on their own character and exertions for their support and station in society are liable in the early part of their career. Every case that I was called on to attend was magnified in my estimation as if my future success had been involved in the result. But such anxieties were transitory, and, on the whole, interfered very little with the comfort of my life.

About this time I became a member of a society which was formed under the name of 'The Animal Chemistry Club,' or 'A Society for the Promotion of Animal Chemistry.' We met at dinner alternately at the houses of Mr. Home and Mr. Hatchett, once in three months, our party consisting of Mr. Home, Mr. Hatchett, Mr. (afterwards Sir Humphry) Davy, Dr. Babington, Mr. William Brande, Mr. Clift, Mr. Children, Dr. Warren, and myself. They were very rational meetings, in which a good deal of scientific discussion was mixed up with lively and agreeable conversation. The society continued to exist for ten or eleven years, but during the latter part of the time, some other members were added to it, and it degenerated into a mere dinner club. Mr. W. Brande and myself are at present the only surviving members. We were, as young men, living on terms of great intimacy, and our friendship has continued unimpaired down to the present time.

Mr. W. Brande was the younger son of Mr. Brande, who had accompanied Queen Charlotte from Germany to England, and was apothecary to the King and Queen and the Royal Household while in London. He had, as a boy, attracted the notice of Mr. Hatchett, and from him had acquired a taste for chemical pursuits. He delivered lectures on chemistry, in connexion with Mr. Wilson's Anatomical School in Great Windmill Street; and was, even at this early period, an excellent lecturer, distinguished for the clearness and method of his discourses, and for the admirable manner in which he performed the experimental part of his instruction. When Sir Humphry Davy, after his marriage with Mrs. Apreece, resigned the Professorship of Chemistry at the Royal Institution, Brande was appointed as his successor, and he continued to hold this office between thirty and forty years. He also succeeded Davy as one of the secretaries of the Royal Society, which office he held for many years, being succeeded by Mr.

Children.   In the early part of his career he
entered on some original investigations in chemistry, and pursued them with much success.
His friends have much regretted that he did not
continue to distinguish himself in this manner
afterwards.   It is, however, easy to be explained.
He married Mr. Hatchett's youngest daughter.
He had a large family, and had abundance of
occupation in his endeavours to obtain the income which, in his condition of life, was necessary to maintain them.   He held an office, which
he holds still, in the Royal Mint.   He held another office as director of the laboratory belonging to the Society of Apothecaries.   He delivered an annual course of lectures, as Professor
of the Royal Institution, and he also delivered
a lecture three mornings in the week, during
the winter, in the laboratory of the Institution ; forming an extended course of chemistry,
which was attended by the medical students of
St. George's Hospital, and by many others, and
which made a constant exertion necessary to
keep him on a level with the increasing knowledge of the day.   In fact, his life was one of

incessant labour, and he had no leisure for other pursuits. If Davy or Faraday had had large families to provide for, they would not have had sufficient leisure, nor sufficient freedom from anxiety, to distinguish themselves as they have done in the line of original research.

The meetings of the Animal Chemistry Club, while it was limited to its original members, were to me very interesting and instructive. Hatchett, who had now inherited a considerable fortune on the death of his father, had ceased to work in chemistry (in spite of the remonstrance of Sir Joseph Banks, who used to say to him in his rough way that 'he would find being a gentleman of fortune was a confounded bad trade'), but he had previously laid up a large store of knowledge, abounded in the materials of conversation, and was a delightful companion. Davy, who in general society was generally over-anxious to display himself to advantage and thought too much of what others would think of him, with us retained his original simplicity, and was quite at his ease. Whatever was the subject of conversation, he

had something to offer and something to sug-
gest, which showed in how remarkable a degree
he combined within himself a highly poetical
imagination with a strict, cautious, and accurate
judgment.   Babington, the intimate friend of
Davy, to whom he dedicated his ' Salmonia,'
with a good deal of scientific knowledge, was
full of the most kind and generous feelings,
and his conversation was enlivened by appropriate anecdotes, with a fund, I will not say of
wit, but of infinite humour.   Home, besides his
acquirements as a naturalist and comparative
anatomist, possessed a knowledge of the world
and of human nature which, displaying itself
every now and then, and without premeditation,
afforded much useful information to younger
men ; otherwise he was no great master of the
art of conversation, or at least not at all to be
compared in this respect to either Hatchett or
Davy.

I may take this opportunity of mentioning an-
other society to which I at this time belonged.
It was founded in the year 1793, by John
Hunter and Dr. Fordyce, under the name of

a 'Society for the Promotion of Medical and Chirurgical Knowledge.' It was originally composed of nine members, with a provision that it might be increased to twelve, but that it should never exceed that number. When they were so kind as to elect me into it, in 1808, Fordyce, John Hunter, and Dr. John Hunter, three of the original members, had been removed from it by death. The existing members were Dr. Baillie, Mr. Home, Dr. (afterwards Sir Gilbert) Blane, Dr. John Clarke, Dr. Robertson Barclay (a son of Dr. Robertson, the historian), Dr. Wells, Mr. (afterwards Sir Patrick) Macgregor, Mr. Wilson, Dr. David Pitcairn, and Dr. Lister. The society had already published two volumes, and another was being prepared for publication. We met at dinner once in a month (except during the summer) at Slaughter's coffee-house in St. Martin's Lane. The papers communicated were first read, and then discussed and corrected after dinner. Dr. Wells, who acted as secretary, was the most active member, and took a great deal of trouble even in correcting the literary composition of the papers. The third and last

volume of their transactions was published in
the year 1812, and contained one short paper of
very little value contributed by myself. From
this time the society continued to exist merely
as a dining club, Dr. Wells having resigned the
secretaryship, to which, though it had become
little more than a nominal office, I succeeded.
The meetings, however, were very regularly attended, and were, to myself at least, very useful
and instructive. In the year 1817, Dr. Wells,
who had always been a person of delicate health,
became affected with a serious illness, which
after some months terminated fatally. Not long
before his death, he addressed, through me, a
letter to the Society, which I still possess, pro-
posing, as it was not probable that they would
ever publish another volume, that the Society
should be dissolved. I suspect that he was
apprehensive that, if it continued to exist, its
future volumes would not maintain the reputation of those which had preceded them. However that might be, the Society acted on his
suggestion, and on June 2, 1818, the formal
dissolution of it took place, it being agreed that

the book containing the minutes of their proceedings should remain in my hands.

Dr. Wells was one of the most remarkable persons with whom it has been my lot to be personally acquainted. He is too well known by his writings, among which his 'Essay on Dew' deserves more especial notice, for it to be worth while for me to speak of him as a philosopher; but I may venture to give some account of him otherwise. He was never married, but lived by himself, with (I believe) only a single maid-servant, in a small house in Serjeant's Inn, Fleet Street. Although he had paid great attention to his profession, and had ample opportunities of studying it as physician to St. Thomas's Hospital, he had never more than a very limited practice. For this, indeed, he was in many respects very unfit: having dry and, in general society, ungracious manners, and being apt to take offence where no offence was intended. Yet he had great kindness and warmth of heart mixed up with these less amiable qualities, and while he was greatly respected by those who really knew him, he was even beloved by the very few with whom he was intimate. His autobiography, which is prefixed to the posthumous edition of his works, is very characteristic, and, when I read it, reminded me very much of that of David Hume, to whom, indeed, as to the character of his intellect, he bore a considerable resemblance, however different he may have been from him in some other respects.

In the course of the year 1812, I communicated to the Royal Society two other papers: one being a continuation of my paper on Poisons; the other containing an account of some further experiments illustrating the influence of the nervous system on the production of animal heat. My former paper on this subject had been very incomplete, inasmuch as I had made no examination of the air expired with reference to the consumption of oxygen and the generation of carbonic acid. In my second series of experiments I endeavoured to supply this deficiency. The experiments were made by means of a very simple apparatus, which fully answered the intended purpose, and were conducted with the greatest care, the expired air being examined by my friend Brande. Although the conclusions which I had ventured to draw from my first series of experiments were certainly premature, they were fully confirmed by my subsequent observations. They have since been further confirmed by those of Le Gallois, as I have shown in the notes which are appended to the republication of my physiological papers in the year 1850.

During this time my private practice was slowly increasing at the rate of about 200*l*. or 250*l*. annually. I continued to pursue my physiological investigations, but was chiefly occupied with the business of the hospital; with taking and arranging my notes of cases, and with adding to my lectures on surgery whatever additional information I had acquired.

During the time of my being house surgeon of the hospital, I had the opportunity of examining, by dissection, a case of what has been called 'spontaneous dislocation of the hip,' consequent on disease of that joint. It very much excited my interest at the time, and led me to speculate

H

on the pathological changes which occur in other cases of disease of the joints. I read and studied all the known works on the subject, but obtained from them no satisfactory information. The treatment of these diseases was, at this time, as unscientific as possible. Different surgeons had different nostrums, which they applied as it happened, without any definite rules as to their application. It occurred to me that there was no department of surgery which more required further investigation than this, or which admitted of greater improvement. From the time of my being elected assistant-surgeon to the hospital, I took notes of almost every case of affection of the joints which occurred among my own patients, and of very many of those which were under the care of the other surgeons. Besides the dissections which I obtained in the hospital, my acquaintance with medical men afforded me the opportunity of making many dissections elsewhere. For a long time I arrived at no results. All was confusion. At the end of the first year I seemed to be no wiser than I had been at the beginning; and at the end of the second I knew little more than at the end of the first. Still I persevered, until at last I perceived some glimmering of light. I had been especially anxious to make the examination of joints in which disease was in its incipient stage. But the opportunities of doing so could present themselves only where patients thus affected had been the victims of other complaints, and were comparatively rare. By constantly looking for them, however, I obtained many such opportunities at last, and then I was enabled to understand many cases of disease in its more advanced stage, which I never could have understood otherwise. In the year 1813 I had made sufficient progress in these enquiries to venture to draw up a paper, which I communicated to the Medical and Chirurgical Society under the title of 'Pathological Researches respecting the Diseases of Joints.' This paper was printed in the fifth volume of the 'Medico-Chirurgical Transactions,' and was the foundation of the volume which I published on the same subject some years afterwards. This work has now gone through five editions. In every succeeding edition I have made such alterations and additions

as were suggested to me by my increased experience; my object being especially to make it
useful to practitioners whose business it is not
merely to understand the exact nature of diseases,
but also to cure them.   I have reason to believe
that my labours have not been in vain, and that
a great number of limbs are now preserved which
would in former times have been amputated as
a matter of course.   Still, I am well aware that
much yet remains to be done, and that it cannot
be otherwise than that, in the course of time, I
must be left behind by those who begin their
enquiries where mine have terminated.   So,
however, it must be in all matters within the
range of the physical sciences.   Whatever we
may learn, there is something to be learned further still; and if this be the case as to chemistry
or physiology, much more must it be so as to so
difficult a science as Pathology, in the pursuit of
which we get little or no help from experiments,
and have to rely almost wholly on the observation of facts which present themselves as it were
incidentally.

In the year 1813 I communicated a paper to

the Royal Society 'On the Influence of the Nervous System on the Action of the Muscles in general, and of the Heart in particular.' It was in the form of the Croonian Lecture, which I had been appointed to deliver by the President.

The doctrine of the schools on these subjects at this time was that of Haller, namely, that the generation of muscular irritability is independent of the nervous system; and that the blood circulating through its cavities is the stimulus on which the contraction of the heart immediately depends. Some doubt had been thrown on the correctness of the last of these opinions by the observations of Le Gallois, who came to the conclusion that the heart derives its force and power of contraction from the spinal cord. It had been shown by Bichat, and the fact had been confirmed by my own experiments, that in warm-blooded animals the heart continues to act so as to maintain the circulation of the venous or dark-coloured blood during a period of two or three minutes after respiration has ceased. In the investigation which formed the subject of the Croonian Lecture, I found that the heart, when suddenly and completely emptied of blood, continued to act even for a longer time than when it remained with its cavities distended with dark-coloured blood after the cessation of respiration; the contractions of the different parts of it being as regular, as orderly, and as vigorous when the circulation is still going on. From this and other circumstances I was led, *first*, to reject the hypothesis of Haller, and to refer the contractions of the heart to the nervous influence supplied by the cardiac plexus of nerves, and not to the stimulus of the blood in its cavities, and *secondly*, to apply the same explanation to the movements of other involuntary muscles. The Council of the Royal Society directed that my paper should be printed in the 'Philosophical Transactions.' On further consideration, however, I was led to request that the printing of it should be postponed, as I felt that the subject required further consideration, and it still remains as one of the unpublished papers in the archives of the Society. My other avocations have prevented my pursuing these enquiries further. But other physiologists, though not exactly on the same grounds, have arrived at the same conclusions; and the anatomical discovery that the grey matter of the nervous system, in which it is supposed that the nervous influence is generated, exists in combination with the cardiac nerves, sufficiently explains some of the phenomena of which I was unable to give a satisfactory explanation formerly.*

During the session of 1808-9, and the three following winters, I had continued to deliver a considerable part of the anatomical lectures in conjunction with Mr. Wilson. In the spring of 1812, however, Mr. Wilson informed me that his increasing practice as a surgeon made it convenient for him to give up his occupation as a teacher of anatomy; and he proposed to me that I should take the anatomical school altogether off his hands, giving him 7,000l. for his anatomical museum and buildings in Great Windmill Street, including the house attached to them, in which he resided, and which had

* The Council of the Royal Society have allowed Mr. C. Hawkins to copy this paper, and it will be published in the complete edition of the Author's Works.

formerly been the residence of William Hunter, and then of his nephew Dr. Baillie. But I had no money of my own at my disposal, and even if my friends could and would have assisted me, I had little disposition to lay myself under such an obligation. I had at that time a very intimate friend, Dr. Harrison, who, like many others of my early friends, has long since been no more (a very zealous person in the pursuit of his profession and the sciences connected with it), and he suggested that we might establish ourselves conjointly as lecturers in anatomy elsewhere. This we might very easily have done and there is little doubt that we should have succeeded in the speculation; for Harrison was very energetic in whatever he undertook, and I had myself become very popular with the students. In saying this I do not at all mean to compare myself as a teacher of anatomy with Mr. Wilson, who, in that capacity, was really pre-eminent; but I had made my anatomical instructions useful by applying them to the explanation of surgical practice, and I had paid more attention than Mr. Wilson had done to physiology, having on this subject a good deal of original matter to communicate, founded on my own observations. I had, however, good reasons for not acceding to this proposal. It would have been very ungracious towards Mr. Wilson, who had always treated me with much kindness, and such a step on my part would have made it difficult for him to dispose of his interest in the Windmill Street School to any one else; and I had myself abundant occupation besides afforded me in the performance of my duties at the hospital and as a lecturer on surgery. Having consulted Dr. Baillie and Sir Everard Home on the subject, I found that their advice corresponded with my own inclinations; and I therefore communicated to Mr. Wilson, *first*, that I must decline the offer which he had made me, and *secondly*, that I would not stand in the way of his making the arrangement which he wished to make with some other person, and that I would willingly retire whenever he had done so. The result was that Sir Charles Bell purchased Mr. Wilson's museum, and took my place as a lecturer on anatomy.

I had been engaged as a teacher of anatomy for seven years, passing always a part of each day in the dissecting-room. Thus I had become very familiar with the subject, so that the impressions made on my mind, and repeated over and over again at a period of life when the memory is in its greatest vigour, have never since become erased. Even at the present day, after the lapse of forty years, I retain all the anatomical knowledge which is required for the purposes of professional practice; and I have little doubt that if I were to return for a short time to the labours of the dissecting-room, I should have no difficulty in resuming my early duties as a demonstrator of anatomy. I have, therefore, nothing to regret in having ceased to be an anatomical teacher; while I am at the same time aware that if I had done otherwise I should not have been able to obtain so extensive a knowledge of diseases and of surgical treatment as I now possess.

During the two or three following years my recollection furnishes me with very little which is worthy of being recorded even in this egotistical memoir. My mode of life was uniform enough. I was constant in my attendance at the hospital, not only doing what was required for the patients, but taking notes of and studying their cases, attending to what little private practice I had obtained, seeing from time to time some of Sir Everard Home's patients when he required assistance or was out of the way, assisting him in dissections in comparative anatomy, and reading some professional books, not in any very systematic way, but for the most part using them for the purpose of reference, as the occasion required. At the same time, though there was little variety in my pursuits, my life was by no means monotonous. I had the advantage of a good deal of agreeable society, and in addition to those whom I have already mentioned, had acquired some valuable friends. Among these I may especially mention Sir Thomas Plumer, who, when I first knew him, held the office of Attorney-General, and afterwards that of Vice-Chancellor and Master of the Rolls. There was as much friendship between us as there could be between a very young man who was working his way upwards, and another nearly thirty years more advanced in life; and from him and his family I received the most constant kindness and attention until the period of his death, in the year 1823.

I am not certain whether it was in 1814 or 1815 that I first became acquainted with the late Lord and Lady Holland. As I have already mentioned, Lord Holland's father had been my own father's friend and patron, to whom he was indebted for the only church preferment which he possessed. My brother-in-law, Marsh, had been Lord Holland's tutor at Christ Church, had afterwards travelled with him on the Continent, and become from that period his most intimate friend. It so happened that Lord Holland had been admitted as a Fellow of the Royal Society on the Thursday after the anniversary on which I received the Copley medal, and when the address made by Sir Joseph Banks to me on that occasion was read as a part of the minutes. It was, I suppose, from this combination of circumstances that I was afterwards invited to Holland House.

By degrees I became a frequent visitor there, and was on terms of much intimacy with Lord Holland until he died, in 1840, and with Lady Holland afterwards. I know not how it was that they liked me at first so well as they did, for in general society I was at this time, and for some years afterwards, a shy and diffident young man, contributing very little to conversation, and not feeling myself at home among the politicians and persons of rank who met at Holland House, as I did among my friends of the Royal Society and those of my own profession or of the law. However, so it was; and their friendship and kindness was never interrupted. Lord Holland was himself one of the kindest of human beings, at the same time being a zealous politician, a thorough Whig, a Liberal in the very best sense of the word, and that not only in politics, but in everything else. Not what used to be called a democrat, but at the same time valuing others more with reference to their general character, talents, and acquirements, than to their rank or station. He was an accomplished scholar, well acquainted with general literature, delighting in

poetry, and of refined taste, but having little
or no acquaintance with science. I remember
dining at Rogers's in company with Sydney
Smith, his brother Robert, and some others,
when a question arose as to who at that time
excelled most in conversation, and they all
agreed that it was Lord Holland. He was indeed in society a most agreeable person, full of
valuable information, which was enlivened by
appropriate anecdotes; not claiming too large a
share of attention for himself; a good listener
as well as a good talker. He had also this excellent quality, that he never spoke ill-naturedly
of others; while he was continually heard to
say, when he thought that others erred a little
in this respect, 'Come, now, I think that you are
a little too hard on him.' He might sometimes
have indulged in some good-humoured sarcasm,
but he never went beyond this. Lady Holland
was a woman of strong sense, with considerable
knowledge of human nature; a zealous and active
friend, but with considerable prejudices. Some
held her to be capricious, but I have certainly
no cause to complain of her in this respect.

Fortunately I had no favours to ask of her or of any one else ; but during thirty years of intimate acquaintance with her, I never knew her miss an opportunity of showing me any small mark of kindness in her power. At Holland House I made some valuable acquaintances; among whom I may especially mention Samuel Rogers, Sydney Smith, and Allen. The latter had originally travelled on the continent with Lord and Lady Holland as their medical attendant. When I knew him he was master of Dulwich College, and resided with them as a friend rather than in any other capacity. He had formerly been a lecturer on physiology in Edinburgh, but afterwards had devoted himself almost entirely to general literature and history. He was a considerable Anglo-Saxon scholar, this being with him a favourite pursuit ; but he had a vast knowledge on all subjects, and was a most instructive companion. At Holland House, also, I became acquainted with Lord Holland's son Charles, now General Fox, and he has continued one of my very best friends down to the present day. Without his literary attainments he has many of his father's qualities—sincere, open, generous—with a character so transparent that whoever knows him must know him thoroughly.

I had previously, although not apparently a very strong person, enjoyed sufficiently good health, and had been able to go through a good deal of rather severe labour; but in the autumn of 1814 my health began to fail. I became dyspeptic, and lost flesh, and altogether looked so ill that many of my acquaintance believed that I laboured under some serious organic disease. I was told of a medical dinner-party in which the question arose as to who would make the next vacancy at St. George's Hospital, and they all agreed that it would be myself. I attribute my illness to unceasing occupation of mind and body for a long period, and partly to having been during ten years in London, never breathing the air of the country for more than two or three days at a time, and even then only on some rare occasions. My indisposition was not sufficient to prevent my attending to my profession as usual; but it depressed my spirits, made

exertion difficult, and my life altogether weari-
some and uncomfortable.   I continued to suffer
—sometimes more, sometimes less—until the
following autumn, when I went, accompanied by
my friend Brande, for a short time to the seaside.   It was remarkable how much, and what
immediate refreshment this change of air and
freedom of labour afforded me.   I returned to
London quite an altered person, and had only
an occasional recurrence of my former symptoms
during the following winter.

During the long war in which we were engaged, with only a brief intermission, from 1793
to 1815, we had little or no intercourse with
scientific or professional men of other countries.
On the conclusion of the war, however, several
of our *collaborateurs* on the Continent visited
this country, with some of whom I became well
acquainted.   Among these were Roux (who was
at that time surgeon to the Hôpital de la Charité,
and who afterwards succeeded to the same office
in the Hôtel Dieu, and was for many years the
principal surgeon of Paris), Orfila, and Magendie

I

and then Ekstrom of Stockholm, Wagner, and others from Germany. There was a Milanese professor, Assalini, who had been with Napoleon in Egypt and Russia, was present at the burning of Moscow, and used to give us some curious details of what occurred in those expeditions. Dupuytren was here only once, and that some years afterwards, when he came to be present at a marriage in the Rothschild family. Among the men of science not immediately connected with the medical profession, those whom I knew best were Blainville and Berzelius. I saw Humboldt only on two occasions, once at Sir Joseph Bank's *soirée*, and once at the Royal Society. On the last occasion I walked back with him to the west end of the town from Somerset House, and I remember that he talked without intermission, displaying an immense store of knowledge, but passing from one subject to another, often without there seeming to be any very due connection between them. When I afterwards read that very remarkable, but rather unreadable production of his later years, ' Cosmos,' it reminded me very forcibly of the conversation

I had with him, or rather which he had with me, more than thirty years previously.

In what I am now writing I do not pretend to give an account of my domestic life; I must not, however, omit to notice the most important event belonging to it, and which must have exercised a great influence over my professional life also, which occurred in the year 1816. Serjeant Sellon, who had been a barrister of a good deal of repute, and well known to lawyers as the author of 'Sellon's Practice,' a work much valued by the legal profession, had been for some years a friend of my elder brother, and through him I became acquainted with the Serjeant's family. His third daughter and myself became much attached to each other; and in the spring of the year above mentioned she became my wife. She was nineteen years of age, and I had not quite completed my thirty-third year. At the time at which I am now writing (1855), we have been married nearly thirty-nine years, and our affection for each other has remained unaltered. She has been an excellent wife to myself, and an excellent mother to our three surviving children. That they have turned out such worthy members of society, and have been a source of so much happiness to ourselves, is to be attributed mainly to the trouble which she took from the very earliest period of their lives in training their moral character, at a time when I was too much engaged in my professional duties to be able to pay the necessary degree of attention to them myself.   What has occurred in my own family confirms the opinion which I might, indeed, have been led to form from what I have seen else-where, that the characters of individuals depend much more on the mother than on the father, the mother having the chief management of them during childhood, when the mind is more pliant, and when permanent habits are more easily established than is the case in after years.

It may be worth while to mention that, in the year of my marriage, my professional income, derived from professional fees and lectures, amounted to 1,530*l.* I had previously saved sufficient money to re-furnish and paint my house, and in other ways make it more fit than it had been before for the reception of a bride. I now, for the first time, had a carriage and a pair of horses. In other respects, we made very little addition to my former establishment. As my wife had no fortune given her at the time of our marriage, nor indeed any except what had been settled on her after her father's and mother's deaths, and as my profession entailed some expenses on us, we were under the necessity of being careful as to our mode of living. My dear wife had no expensive habits, and we managed to make both ends meet at the end of the year. Still, I cannot but say that this was a period of considerable anxiety, when I felt for the first time that another individual as well as myself, and probably children hereafter, had to depend, not only on my professional character, but also on my bodily health. Fortunately, in the beginning of the following year there was a more manifest increase of my practice than there had ever been before. This kept my anxiety within bounds; still it was considerable, and was probably the cause of my having some return of the dyspeptic symptoms under which I had laboured formerly, and which continued to trouble me, from time to time, for the two or three following years.

Although, between my increasing practice, my duties at the hospital, and my lectures, my time was considerably more occupied than formerly, I nevertheless found some leisure for the cultivation of physiology. It was at this time that I made the experiment of passing a ligature round the choledoch duct, of which I afterwards published an account in ' Brande's Journal.' The conclusion at which I arrived was, that the interruption of the flow of the bile into the intestine stopped the formation of chyle. The experiment was repeated by Herbert Mayo in London, and Macartney in Dublin, with the same result. Dr. Blundell, who was at that time lecturing on Physiology at Guy's Hospital, made the same experiment, not knowing that I had made it previously, and he also arrived at the same conclusion. When I afterwards published my statement, Dr. Blundell complained to Mr. Green that I had robbed him of his discovery. This led to a comparison of dates, and it turned out that my first successful experiment had been made just three weeks before his. Since then Tiedemann and Bernard have repeated the experiment, and, as they declare, with a different result; the latter being of opinion that it is the secretion of the pancreas, and not that of the liver, which is the principal agent of chylification. M. Bernard is led to believe that the disagreement between his experiment and mine is to be explained by my having included the duct of the pancreas in the same ligature with the choledoch duct. Other engagements have prevented my prosecuting the inquiry further. I am, however, far from being convinced that Mayo, Macartney, Blundell, and myself, have been in an error. I do not find that the other experimentalists paid attention to the contents of the intestine after the flow of bile had been suspended. If they had done so, they could not have failed to remark the very striking difference which there is in them where the bile does not flow into the intestine, as compared with that which exists where the flow of bile has not been interrupted.

In the two or three years which followed my marriage I find little worth recording. My eldest son was born in the winter of 1817. In 1818 we had another child, a little boy, who was named Alexander, after my kind friend Mr. Alexander Brodie, father of the present Duchess of Gordon. Our little Alexander, however, was taken from us when he was about a year old. Our daughter was born in the following year, and our youngest son in the autumn of 1821. We have had no other children.

It was in the year 1817 or 1818 that I first formed a rather intimate acquaintance with the late Sir William Knighton. In the year 1815 Sir William was in attendance on the Duke of ——, in a very serious attack of illness which terminated fatally. I was applied to for the purpose of examining the body after death. Some foolish or ill-disposed persons had persuaded the Duchess that Knighton had mistaken the nature of the Duke's complaint, and that he had treated him improperly. The examination which I made proved that this charge was altogether unfounded. After I had sent

my written report the Duchess asked me to call
upon her, and she and her sister cross-examined
me on the subject, being, as it appeared to me,
very ready to attribute blame to the physician.
I took his part, as it was my duty to do, and
believed that I had satisfied them that the
opinion which they had been led to form was
erroneous. Not a word ever passed between
Knighton and myself on the subject. But from
this time he became one of my warmest and
kindest friends. As his history is somewhat remarkable, I think it worth while to take this
opportunity of giving some account of it.

He was of humble origin, and I believe that
he had originally practised for a short time as an
apothecary at Plymouth. While there, he married the present Dowager Lady Knighton. She
was a Miss Hawker, and one of a family of great
respectability well known in Devonshire; being
herself a very superior person both morally and
intellectually, and highly accomplished. After
his marriage Mr. Knighton went to Edinburgh,
studied there, and graduated as a physician.
He then came to London, took a house in
Maddox Street, and engaged in practice as a

physician and accoucheur. He had at first few friends; but he was ambitious and determined to succeed. He devoted himself wholly to his profession, being always to be found, and not at all mixing in general society. With great natural sagacity, he had most agreeable and engaging manners, and the result was that in the course of a very few years he obtained a very large practice. During the war he accompianed the Marquis Wellesley when he went on a temporary diplomatic mission to Spain. On his return to England Lord Wellesley introduced him to the Prince Regent, and soon afterwards he was created a baronet.

According to common report, which I believe in this instance to have been well founded, an accidental circumstance led to his being more intimately acquainted with the Regent. M'Mahon, who at that time held the office of Keeper of the Privy Purse, died, and in his will named Knighton as his executor. Among the papers of the deceased were found some which belonged to the Regent, which ought to have been destroyed. Knighton at once took the papers to the Regent, and from that time was his friend, exercising a considerable influence over him. I do not pretend to unravel the mysteries of a court, but of this I feel assured, that however much the production of the papers might have contributed to it in the first instance, he was indebted for the long continuance of the Regent's favour more to his engaging manners, his knowledge of the world, his habits of business, and his usefulness, than to anything else. When Sir Benjamin Bloomfield (who after M'Mahon was Keeper of the Privy Purse) was made a peer, and became our minister at Stockholm, Knighton was appointed to succeed him, and he retained his office until the death of his master in 1830.

Knighton was a man of considerable natural powers. He had great sagacity, a very clear head, and an excellent judgment, seeing at once the main points of the question before him, divested of those which were of no real importance. He was one of that very limited class of persons who have great influence over the minds of others. This may be attributed in part to his engaging manners, but more to the circumstance that he entered, or seemed to enter, into the views and interests of those for whom he entertained a regard as cordially as if they were his own. Having been originally imperfectly educated, he was deficient in some of the qualities which would have fitted him for general society, but these defects were more than compensated by his ready insight into the characters of other men, and his knowledge of the world and of what goes on in the world. In his profession, with much practical knowledge, he had no scientific attainments. He pursued it in the first instance with no other object than that of obtaining a livelihood, and afterwards with a too great anxiety to amass a fortune. This was his principal failing, and in the latter part of his life he acknowledged to me that he was conscious that it had been so. The existence of it in his case, as in that of many others, is to be explained by the circumstance of his having passed his early years in poverty, contending with difficulties, but with very ambitious aspirations.

When the Regent first proposed to him that he should belong to his household, Lady Knighton very much objected to his doing so. At first, and for several years after his master succeeded to the crown, everything went on smoothly. He was very useful, and the King's private affairs were managed in a way in which they had never been managed previously. His situation became very disagreeable, and, as he informed me, he wished to resign his office. But Lady Knighton showed him that, having once undertaken it, he could not with propriety do so, especially as he still retained the King's confidence, as was shown by his relying on his advice, and by his leaving him his executor, in conjunction with the Duke of Wellington. On the whole, I am satisfied that he would have been a happier person if he had never entered on this new career. It is worthy of notice that he studiously avoided leading his family to follow his example. I do not believe that either Lady Knighton, or his son, or daughters, were ever presented at Court. After the death of the King he mixed little with the world, leading a very retired life at his residence in Hampshire. He survived the King only six years, and Sir Steven Hammick, Dr. Chambers, myself, and one other friend, were the only persons, besides his son, who attended his funeral at the cemetery at Kensal Green.

In the year 1818 I experienced the loss of a very good friend by the death of Sir Richard Croft. He had married my first cousin, one of the daughters of Dr. Denman, and was from an early period of his life in large practice as an accoucheur among the aristocratic classes of society. Unfortunately he was engaged to attend the Princess Charlotte of Wales in her confinement. The child was born dead, and the princess herself expired soon after her delivery. This disastrous result affected him deeply. Sir Richard was a man of acute feelings, a thorough gentleman, having a high sense of honour, and of a kind and liberal disposition. In the early part of my career he did me much service by recommending me to his patients for those smaller services for which they might reasonably apply to a young practitioner. He was the younger son of an old family whose fortune had evaporated. On the death of his elder brother, Sir Herbert Croft, he succeeded to one of the oldest baronetcies, and to nothing else.

During the first two or three years after our marriage we continued to reside in the small house in Sackville Street, in which I had resided previously. In the beginning of the year 1819, however, I took a house of greater pretensions in Savile Row, and we remained in it until we removed to a larger one in the same street, which we still inhabit. As my income had been steadily increasing, I felt myself to be guilty of no imprudence in making this change, and the event justified me in doing so, as my income in 1819 exceeded that of the previous year by more than 1,000*l.* This increase may be in part attributed to the publication of the first edition of my work on 'Diseases of the Joints,' which had taken place in the previous year. Other circumstances, however, contributed to it. Although I was no more than thirty-six years of age, my name had been for several years before the public. Sir Astley Cooper, who had succeeded to the large practice of Mr. Cline and the smaller one of Sir Everard Home, too confident of his position, had already begun to lose some of the vast reputation which he had previously enjoyed. Some one else was wanted, and I was ready to fill the vacant place. From this time my practice steadily increased, so that almost every year made considerable additions to it. Hitherto my income had been little more than sufficient to meet my annual expenditure, but I now began to lay by a considerable portion of it; and finding that I had the prospect of providing for my family, and of acquiring in the course of no very long time a moderate independence, I was relieved of much of the anxiety which I had formerly experienced.

In the same year in which I entered my new habitation, 1819, Lawrence having resigned the Professorship of Comparative Anatomy and Physiology at the College of Surgeons, the council of the college appointed me to succeed him, and I delivered my first course of lectures there in the year following. I do not know whether I acted quite wisely in undertaking that office.

With an increasing practice, my lectures on surgery, and my duties at the hospital, I had an abundance of occupation, and the having every year to make a fresh course of lectures on subjects on which I had not lectured previously was an almost frightful addition to my labours. It was only by giving up many hours which ought to have been devoted to sleep that I was able to fulfil my engagements, and even with this sacrifice I had not the satisfaction of knowing that my lectures were such as I could have wished them to be. On the other hand, in the composition of my lectures I had to go to the bottom of many things with which I was before only superficially acquainted, and thus I acquired much information which I should never have possessed otherwise, and which has been a source of interest to me ever since. I held the professorship until the year 1823, and delivered four courses of lectures. The two first courses related to the structure and physiology of the organs of respiration and circulation. In the third course I considered the organs of digestion; the subject of the last course

K

being the anatomy and functions of the nervous system.

I may take this opportunity of observing that I have found few things to contribute more to my own improvement than the composition of my lectures, and the habit otherwise of recording my knowledge and thoughts in writing. It has enabled me to detect my own deficiencies, to avoid hasty conclusions, and has taught me to be less conceited of my own opinions than I should have been otherwise. Another result has been to give many things a permanent place in my memory, the impressions of which, without such artificial help, would have been evanescent. In the early part of my life I was accustomed to make written notes of books which I read, a few of which are still preserved among my papers, and I refer to them with no small degree of satisfaction as having rendered me an important service.

It was in the year 1821, and while I held the office of professor at the College of Surgeons, that I was first called on to attend the King, George IV., under the following circumstances.

His Majesty had one of the common encysted tumours which occur on the scalp, which was large enough to be troublesome to him. He showed it to Sir Everard Home, who advised him to have it removed by an operation. The King was anxious to undergo the operation. His Majesty, however, expressed to Sir William Knighton that he wished the operation to be performed by myself, Sir Everard being, however, present, and Knighton was commissioned to make this communication to me. I cannot say that I derived any particular satisfaction from it, as I found that I had already obtained the patronage of the public, and was quite contented with it. In the meanwhile, however, the subject of the proposed operation was mentioned to Lord Liverpool, who was then prime minister. Lord Liverpool represented to the King that it was a matter which might concern the public as well as himself, and urged that nothing should be done without Sir Astley (then Mr.) Cooper being first consulted, and that, if an operation was determined on, Sir Astley should perform it. Sir Astley being at that time the

most conspicuous person in his profession, I cannot doubt that Lord Liverpool's judgment was
quite correct.   Accordingly, Sir Everard Home,
Sir Astley Cooper, and myself were summoned
to Windsor; when, after examining the tumour,
we agreed that nothing but an operation could be
of any service, and that it should be performed
when the King returned to London.   Mr. Cline
was consulted afterwards, who confirmed the
opinion which we had given.   Eventually the
operation was performed by Sir Astley Cooper,
in the presence of Sir Everard Home, Mr. Cline
Sir William Knighton, the King's physicians,
Sir Henry Halford, Sir Mathew Tierney, and
myself, making indeed a very large assembly for
so small a matter.   After this attendance, Cooper
was created a baronet, and Sir Everard Home,
was comforted by being appointed to the office
of surgeon to Chelsea Hospital, vacated by the
death of Mr. Thomas Keate, and by his son,
who was then a very young lieutenant in the
navy, being advanced rather prematurely t the
rank of commander.   From this time, when any
surgical operation was required, the King, for

some years, was in the habit of applying to
Cooper; but on some special occasions I was
summoned to meet him in consultation, though
I held no actual appointment in the royal household until the year 1828, when, on Sir Astley
having been appointed Serjeant-Surgeon, I was
gazetted as surgeon to his Majesty's person in
his place.

In the year 1822, Mr. Griffiths, one of the
principal surgeons of St. George's Hospital,
having been compelled by ill-health to resign
his office, I was, as might have been anticipated,
elected without any opposition as his successor.
For many years after my first being appointed
assistant-surgeon, Sir Everard had very little
interfered with the management of his patients,
and from this circumstance, and from that of
my having had for many years the charge of
Mr. Gunning's patients during his absence in
the Peninsula, I had abundant opportunities of
improving myself in my profession.

In the early part of the year 1823 I sustained
a severe loss by the death of my affectionate

friend Sir Thomas Plumer, who sank at last
under the influence of a local disease, which had
tormented him for fourteen or fifteen years; but
which, nevertheless, had not interfered with the
able and conscientious discharge of his duties
as Solicitor-General, Attorney-General, Vice-
Chancellor, and Master of the Rolls, which last
situation he occupied at the time of his death.
As I have already mentioned, I had been intimately acquainted with him and his family for
eleven or twelve years, had been his frequent
visitor at Canons Park, where he resided during his vacations, and had received from him
such undeviating kindness and attention as
could not but be very acceptable to a young
man who was labouring to make his way in a
profession, without having as yet reaped the advantage of his labours.

In the autumn of the same year the medical
profession was deprived of one who for many
years had occupied perhaps the most conspicuous
place in it, and was indeed one of its brightest
ornaments, by the death of Dr. Baillie. I have
already mentioned that he had married my first

cousin, one of the daughters of Dr. Denman. In consequence of this connection, I had the opportunity of becoming well acquainted with him.

The nephew of William Hunter, he had, on his uncle's death, and at a very early period of life, become established as the principal lecturer in the then famous Anatomical School of Great Windmill Street. He had left off teaching anatomy two or three years before I began my studies in London, and after another year he had resigned his office as physician to St. George's Hospital, so that I had no opportunity of personally knowing him as a teacher either in one place or in the other. That he was excellent as a lecturer is proved by his large and constantly increasing class, and by the high estimation in which he was always held by those who had been his pupils. In the beginning of the present century, being then about forty years of age, he had acquired a very considerable share of private practice, which rapidly increased, until it exceeded in extent not only that of any one among his contemporaries, but probably of any other physician who had preceded him since the days of Radcliffe and Mead. His reputation was of the highest order, as it depended on the opinion entertained of him by the members of his own profession, who always looked up to him as the fittest person to be consulted in cases of difficulty or danger. Their preference of him is to be attributed partly to his knowledge and sagacity, especially in what related to the diagnosis of disease, and partly to his general character, which led him to be always liberal and considerate as to others, at the same time that he never seemed to be anxious about his own reputation, or to take any trouble to obtain peculiar credit for himself. He had also another important qualification for the situation of a consulting physician. He not only had a very clear perception of the matter which was placed before him, distinguishing at once that which was essential from that which was merely incidental; but his habit of lecturing had given him a considerable command of language, which enabled him to explain even a complicated case in the way which was satisfactory to the patient and his friends.   In these explanations he never gave his knowledge for more than it was worth, nor pretended to know more than he knew in reality; and this simple and straightforward mode of proceeding was one reason why the public reposed in him a degree of confidence which those of more ambitious pretensions were wholly unable to attain.

Being the only physician of that time who had been engaged in teaching anatomy, the public naturally, and very justly, considered that he must have some knowledge of disease which others, in his department of the profession, did not possess.   But this was not all. Bred up in W. Hunter's museum, of which the anatomy of diseased structures formed an important part, and having had ample opportunities of investigating disease by dissections at St. George's Hospital, he had become, after his uncles, William and John Hunter, the most distinguished pathologist of the day.   His work on 'Morbid Anatomy,' which he had published while comparatively a young man, is still the most valuable textbook on that subject that

exists.   Very much has been added to the knowledge which it contains by the labours of later
pathologists, and the use of the achromatic mi-
croscope has added another kind of investigation to that which was adopted formerly: still,
it is perfect as far as it goes; and the clearness,
conciseness, and simplicity of the style, and the
brief but accurate sketches of the symptoms
during life, which are appended to the account
of the appearances after death, have the effect
of rendering it a more important help to the
practitioner (whose object is to recognize the
diseases which come before him, and not merely
to study pathology as a curious science), than
most of the more elaborate treatises which have
been since published.

As a contributor to medical literature, Baillie's
reputation rests almost wholly on the work of
which I have now been speaking.   He published, however, a few rather interesting, but
not very important papers in the " Transactions
of a Society for the Improvement of Medical
and Chirurgical Knowledge."   It would be un-
fair to measure his reputation by some papers

which were published after his death, written during his declining years, when he had outlived the vigour of his intellect.

Baillie was not originally (as I apprehend) a man of great physical powers. It seemed to me that he found exertion, either of body or mind, beyond a certain point always inconvenient and painful. As a young man, he had studied anatomy and physiology, so as to make himself thoroughly qualified for his office as a teacher; but he never went beyond this, nor entered on any original investigation in either of these departments of knowledge. When he was fully engaged in private practice, his labours were very arduous. He rose at six o'clock in the morning, and was occupied until he breakfasted at eight o'clock, in answering the letters of his correspondents; from that time he was employed in seeing patients until six or seven o'clock in the evening, when he returned home to dinner. He had to make another round of professional visits in the evening, and seldom retired to rest much sooner than twelve o'clock. These labours continued for several successive years. At the same time, however, he allowed himself a vacation during the summer, which gradually became prolonged from three weeks to three or four months. Notwithstanding this periodical retirement, he had always the appearance of being overworked. He was nervous and irritable, and while others looked, if not with envy, with some sort of admiration at his large practice, he complained of it as if it were a great hardship, and I have no doubt felt it at the time to be so. His professional brethren had little sympathy with and smiled at these complaints; yet they were well-founded, and I suspect that he would have been a happier man, and have lived longer, if he had had a smaller amount of professional success. For some years before he died he had limited his practice by acting merely as a consulting physician with other physicians or surgeons; at the same time, passing two days in the week in Windsor Castle, taking his turn with the other physicians, who were in attendance on King George III. during the long period of his mental derangement. But he did not make this change until both his mind and body had suffered from the over-exertion of preceding years; and no one who knew him merely towards the close of his career could form a right notion of what he had been formerly. He left to his son a sufficient, but not a large fortune. He might have left a much larger one if he had made it his object to do so. But he had no desire to be rich, and was liberal not only to his patients but to others, performing, as I have reason to believe, many acts of charity and kindness. The irritability of temper, to which I have already referred, led him at times to say hasty and somewhat ungracious things, for which he was always sorry, and apt to worry himself afterwards. Mrs. Baillie was a lady of great good sense, an excellent adviser, and a great help to her husband in a variety of ways.

In the year of which I am now speaking (1823) I had already obtained a considerable private practice, my income from fees alone, independently of what was derived from my surgical lectures and my pupils at the hospital, amounting to £6500. From this time my practice went on for many years steadily increasing ; there being only one year (after the financial crisis of 1825-26)' in which there was any falling off, and this not to any considerable extent.   It was now my object to devote myself as much as possible to my profession, and to take advantage of the favourable opinion of the public, so that I might make a provision for myself and my family.   Accordingly, I never absented myself from London for more than three weeks in the summer, and sometimes not at all.   During the empty season, I engaged at first a ready furnished house at Hampstead, and afterwards had a permanent residence there, at which my family remained, and where I dined and slept, coming to London every morning after an early breakfast.   My receipts were such that I was able every year to lay by a considerable sum of money, so that I had no further anxiety as to the fate of my wife and children, in regard to pecuniary matters, if I should be taken from them.   But I had anxieties of other kinds.   I had now a large share of operative surgery : far more than fell to the lot of any other individual in the metropolis.   Sir Astley Cooper's practice was beginning to decline, and he finally quitted London for a considerable time in the year 1828, and the greater number of patients, who would otherwise have applied to him, now resorted to myself.   I was never much attached to this department of my profession, which I considered as requiring far less of intellectual accomplishments than the diagnosis of disease and the treatment of it in other ways.   However, I could not venture to refuse what was offered to me, and I hope that I did justice to those who reposed confidence in me by sparing neither time nor trouble, and by neglecting nothing that could in any degree contribute to bring a case in which I was engaged to a successful termination.   The only operation that gave me any real concern was that of lithotomy.   Among the affluent classes of society, lithotomy is very rarely required for children, and hence those who form the very great majority of patients in the hospital, form a very small proportion in private practice.   But lithotomy in adults is always dangerous, and among what are called the higher classes of society it is more dangerous than among the labouring classes; as those belonging to the former are apt to defer applying for relief to the last moment, when the extension of disease has made them less fitted to undergo an operation than they would have been at an earlier period. After the year 1835, except in the hospital, I scarcely ever had recourse to lithotomy at all, substituting for it that of lithotrity, of which my experience leads me to believe that, in the hands of one who has taken the necessary pains to understand it, it is attended with less risk as to life than almost any other of the capital operations of surgery.

At the period of which I am now speaking, a great change had gradually taken place in the medical staff of our hospital. Sir Everard Home had resigned the office of surgeon, residing at the house which belonged to him as surgeon of Chelsea College. Mr. Gunning had retired also, and become a resident in Paris. Mr. Robert Keate was now the senior surgeon, Jeffreys and Rose were the two junior surgeons, that is, juniors to myself at the hospital, though my seniors in years. The physicians were Dr. Pearson, Dr. Nevinson, Dr. Chambers, and Dr. Young. Of these, Dr. Nevinson was an excellent practical physician, and had a vast reputation among the members of his own profession. He might with the greatest ease have succeeded to a very large private practice—probably equal to that of Baillie himself. But this formed no part of his ambition, and while he devoted a very large portion of his time not only to the in-patients, but also to the out-patients of the hospital, he seemed to shrink from the more lucrative engagements of his profession. The same could not be said of Dr. Pearson, who, however, never succeeded as a practitioner, except to a very limited extent. In fact, circumstances, combined with various eccentricities, stood in his way, though he was a person of considerable genius, and had obtained a good deal of credit by some papers published in the 'Philosophical Transactions.' Young, one of the greatest philosophers of the age, and indeed second to none but Davy, never prospered as a physician. His biographer, Dr. Peacock, has ascribed his failure to his being too good for his profession, and to his being above certain ignoble arts, which were, as he believed, made use of by his competitors, and he has availed himself of this opportunity of publishing a very illiberal tirade against those who belong to this division of the medical profession. Nothing can be more unjust than the whole of Dr. Peacock's observations on the subject. There may be among physicians, as well as in other professions, some individuals who acquire a reputation to which they have no claim, but my experience justifies me in asserting that no physician acquires a *large* reputation, or retains what may be called an extensive practice, who is really unworthy of it. The public are, on the whole, pretty good judges in a matter in which they are so much interested, and if by any accident they have been led to give their confidence to a wrong person, they are seldom long in discovering and correcting their mistake. With regard to Dr. Young, the truth is that either his mind, from it having been so long trained

by the study of the more exact sciences, was not
fitted for the profession which he had chosen, or
that it was so much engrossed by other, and to
him more interesting pursuits, that he never
bestowed on it that constant and patient attention without which no one can be a great physician, any more than he can be a great surgeon,
or a great lawyer, or a great statesman. The
students at the hospital complained that they
learned nothing from him. I never could dis-
cern that he kept any written notes of cases,
and I doubt whether he ever thought of his
cases in the hospital after he had left the wards.
His medical writings were little more than
compilations from books, with no indications of
original research. I offer these observations as
a matter of justice to others, and not in depreciation of Dr. Young, for whom I had a
great personal regard, whose vast and varied
attainments out of his profession, and whose
great original genius displayed in other ways,
place him in the foremost rank of those whose
names adorn the annals of our country. Dr.
Peacock mentions as a proof of his superiority

as a physician, that the list of his hospital patients presented a larger proportion of cures than that of any of his colleagues. I doubt not that the statement is true, but the conclusion from it is wrong. Hospital patients as well as private patients have their preferences, and those who labour under dangerous diseases will take some trouble to be admitted under the care of the physician or surgeon in whom they repose the greatest confidence; while those whose ailments are less important are contented to take their chance of being admitted under one person or under another. Moreover, many patients are sent to a hospital by private practitioners, and it is no matter of wonder that those who, if they themselves laboured under severe illness, would consult not Young, but Chambers or Nevinson, showed the same preference as to poor persons in whom they were interested.

Of my other colleagues whose names I have mentioned, Dr. Chambers was at that time but little known to the general public. But he was assiduous in his attentions to the hospital, and laying up that store of experience which after-wards enabled him to attain the highest position in his profession. He had great natural sagacity, and a clearness of perception and judgment which enabled him at once to see the important part of whatever subject was placed before him, discarding all irrelevant matter. He had other and, I may say, still higher qualities, which caused him to be very generally popular. He was a gentleman in the best sense of the word: honourable in his dealings with others; kind and affectionate to his friends; using no mean arts to enhance his own reputation or depreciate that of others. To this may be added that he was an accomplished scholar, and having extensive literary attainments. I owe much to the long intimacy which existed between us, and which terminated only with his death. Rose and Jeffreys, though, as I have already stated, my seniors in age, were my juniors in the hospital. Their career was short; the former being taken from us in the year 1829, and the latter in a year or two afterwards.

Although I had been previously consulted by

the King (George IV.), it was only on some
rare occasions.   In the spring of 1830 some
symptoms under which His Majesty had long
laboured, arising from disease in the semilunar
valves of the aorta, became much aggravated,
and thus commenced the illness which terminated in his death some months afterwards, and
during which he was attended by his physicians,
Sir Henry Halford and Sir Matthew Tierney.
It was early in May that Sir William Knighton
called on me one forenoon, and said, ' I have
the King's commands that you should accompany me immediately to Windsor.   They have
got into a difficulty, and you must come and
see if you can help them out of it.'   On my
arrival I found that the King's lower limbs were
dropsical and enormously swollen, and that they
had been scarified with a lancet, the consequence
of which was that the swelling was not at all
relieved, and that they were highly inflamed
and in danger of gangrene; a further delay of
twenty-four hours would probably have placed
him beyond the hope of recovery from this local
mischief.   I at once made a good many punc-

tures with a round needle of the size of that
which is known by the name of a worsted-
needle. This produced an immense discharge
of fluid; and the success of the punctures and
of the other treatment which was continued
with it was complete. In the course of a fortnight not only were the limbs free from inflam-
mation, and reduced to their natural size, but
the state of his chest was so much improved
that, instead of being scarcely able to breathe
except he was in a sitting posture, he could
throw himself on his bed and sleep in a hori-
zontal posture with no other support than a
pillow under his head. His Majesty was not
only sensible of the relief which he thus obtained, but full of expressions of gratitude for
what I had done for him. After the first three
weeks all that I had been especially required to
do was accomplished. He would not, however,
allow me to discontinue my attendance on him.
My habit was to go to Windsor every evening
after an early dinner, sleep in the castle, and
return to London, after a very early breakfast,
in the morning. I generally went to the King's

apartments about six o'clock in the morning, and sat by his bedside for one or two hours before my departure, during which he conversed on various subjects, not unfrequently speculating on his own condition and prospects. In his more sanguine moments his mind would revert to the cottage which he had built at Windsor Park, and he expressed the pleasure which it would afford him to return to this his favourite retreat, as if he had found the comparatively retired life which he led there much more suited to his taste than the splendour of Windsor Castle. The impression made on my mind by the very limited observations which I was able to make on these occasions, was that the King would have been a happier and a better man if it had been his lot to be nothing more than a simple country gentleman, instead of being in the exalted situation which he inherited. If William IV. retained his simplicity of character, and his freedom from selfishness, it was because he ascended the throne at a late period of life, having had no previous expectation that he would ever be thus elevated.

I never attended King William IV. professionally. But I saw him occasionally, when I was visiting the Princess Louise (Queen Adelaide's niece, who was brought over from Germany for the purpose of consulting Sir Astley Cooper and myself), and at some other times. It was, I suppose, from the report made to him of his brother's sentiments towards me, that I found him always most kind and gracious. I have in my possession a letter from Sir Matthew Tierney, giving me an account of a conversation in which the King expressed very strongly his favourable opinion of me, and declared it to be his intention that, if a vacancy occurred in the office of Serjeant-Surgeon, I should have the appointment. He acted on this intention two years afterwards, when I succeeded Sir Everard Home, who had held that office previously.

The office of Serjeant-Surgeon is of very ancient date, and it has generally been confined to those who have been previously engaged in the service of the royal family. It is held under a patent during the life of the patentee, with a moderate salary attached to it; and hence it is that, as I was originally Serjeant-Surgeon to King William, I am now Serjeant-Surgeon to Queen Victoria. Formerly there were some privileges attached to the office, but an alteration in the constitution of the College of Surgeons having been made by charter in the year 1843, the reason for maintaining them ceased to exist, and by my own suggestion they were discontinued.

I have already mentioned that I began the delivery of surgical lectures in the autumn of the year 1808. I continued to deliver them in Mr. Wilson's anatomical theatre until I had retired from the anatomical lectures. I then engaged a house in Great Windmill Street, in which I constructed a theatre for my lectures, reserving the rest of the house for the residence of a porter, and for a museum consisting of preparations illustrative of surgical pathology. With regard to the latter, I was at first contented with the preservation of such specimens as I was able to prepare with my own hands; but as I obtained an increase of income with an increase of occupation, I engaged the services of Dr. James Somerville as my assistant, and thus, in the course of a few years, I became possessed of a collection of preparations which was admirably adapted for the intended purpose of illustrating my lectures. I continued to lecture in my Windmill Street theatre until the year 1829, and then, in compliance with the wishes of my colleagues, I transferred my lectures to the theatre of St. George's Hospital, at the same time presenting my pathological museum to the governors of that institution for the use of the Medical School. It has been gratifying to me to find that not only my original preparations have been carefully preserved, but that large additions have been made to them, so that the Pathological Museum of St. George's Hospital, at the time at which I am now writing, is one of the most valuable and useful collections of the kind in the metropolis.

For many years my lectures formed not only a very useful, but a very interesting addition to my employments. As, however, I became more engaged with private practice, I found the delivery of them three evenings of the week (and always more frequently towards the end of the course) to be very inconvenient. I often had scarcely time to eat a hasty dinner before I proceeded to the lecture-room; and then, almost immediately after my lecture was concluded, had to visit patients who required a second visit during the twenty-four hours, or whom I had been prevented from visiting in the early part of the day. Thus I was unable to begin answering the letters of my correspondents, who were always pretty numerous, until a late hour in the evening; and was generally employed, with little intermission, from half-past eight in the morning until midnight, besides having not unfrequently to make journeys into the country, which occupied a considerable portion of the night. Being thus pressed, I was desirous of retiring from my duties as a lecturer as soon as I had the opportunity of doing so. That opportunity, however, did not occur until the year 1830, when I was enabled to give up my class to my junior colleagues at the hospital, Mr. Cæsar Hawkins and Mr. George Babington.

Although I ceased to deliver a systematic course of surgical lectures, I felt that the students of the hospital had just claims on me for instruction ; and in addition to the explanation which I was always in the habit of giving them at the bedside of the patients, I continued once in a week to deliver clinical lectures in the early part of the day, during a great part of the year ; and probably, with my increased professional experience, was thus able to afford them a greater amount of useful practical information than I should have done if I had confined myself to lectures of the same description as those which I had delivered formerly.

It was in the year 1822 that I published a second edition of my treatise on the Diseases of the Joints. The copies were soon exhausted, and the work was for many years out of print. A third edition, which was, I hope, much improved, was published in the year 1834, and two editions have been published since. In the year 1832 I published my lectures on the Diseases of the Urinary Organs. There was no very practical work on the subject previously, and it

has now reached a fourth edition. My Lectures
illustrative of Local Nervous Diseases were published in 1837. They formed a thin volume,
but I believe that I am not wrong in stating that
none of my publications have been really more
useful to the world than this, preventing a multitude of mistakes which surgeons were apt to
make in confounding mere neuralgic affections
with more serious maladies. These lectures
have now been for several years out of print, it
being my intention, if I live long enough, to re-
publish them, with some others, at some future
period. Though not belonging to this period of
my life, I may here mention that in the year
1847 I published another volume of miscellane-
ous 'Lectures illustrative of various Subjects in
Pathology and Surgery.' Besides these, I communicated various papers on Injuries of the
Brain, Injuries of the Spinal Cord, and other
subjects, to the Royal Medical and Chirurgical
Society, which have appeared at various times
in the Medico-Chirurgical Transactions.

I have formerly referred to my having the appointment of Serjeant-Surgeon conferred on me by his late Majesty. This was on the death of Sir Everard Home, in the year 1832.

Sir Everard had for a long series of years occupied a very prominent place in his profession. No account of him has ever been given to the world, and a brief record of what I know respecting him may not be unacceptable to those who may think it worth while to peruse what I am now writing.

He was one of an old Scotch family, and was rather proud of a genealogy, the details of which, if I ever knew them, have passed out of my recollection. He had two brothers, one of whom I have seen, a colonel in the service of the East India Company, and the other a painter, who practised his profession (chiefly in painting portraits) with great success in Calcutta. One of his sisters was married to John Hunter, another to Mylne, an architect and engineer of great distinction, one of whose works was the bridge over the Thames at Blackfriars. Home was educated at Westminster School, and had been elected from the college there to an exhibition at Cambridge. At this time John Hunter had proposed to his young brother-in-law to have him educated to his own profession, and by the advice of the head master of the school he gave up his exhibition at the University in order that he might at once avail himself of John Hunter's offer.· He studied anatomy at first under William Hunter, and if I am not mistaken, resided for some time in his house, and assisted him by teaching the students in the dissecting-room. Before his education was well-nigh completed, there was some kind of disagreement between him and John Hunter, which led to his entering the army as an assistant-surgeon. In this capacity he was sent to the West Indies. After some time he became reconciled to his brother-in-law, the process of reconciliation having been promoted by his sending him some specimens of natural history, which were not then so easily obtained as they are at present. On his return to England he resided for some years in John Hunter's house, where he assisted him in his scientific researches, and at the same time taught anatomy to a limited number of pupils in a private dissecting-room. One of these pupils was afterwards John Thomson, who when the Whigs came into office with the Grenville party in 1806 was made by them professor of military surgery in Edinburgh. Some time before John Hunter's death, Home was elected assistant-surgeon to St. George's Hospital; and when that event occurred in 1793, he succeeded Hunter as surgeon to that institution.

On the resignation of Mr. Charles Hawkins, he became serjeant-surgeon to the King (George III.), with whom, however, he never had any personal communication. In the year 1812 he was created a baronet. The title is now extinct, his elder son, a captain in the navy, having died in Australia unmarried, and his other son having died two or three years before.

He retained the office of surgeon to St. George's Hospital until the year 1827. On the death of Mr. Keate in 1821, he was appointed surgeon to Chelsea Hospital, where he had an official residence, in which he passed the last few years of his life.

Sir Everard Home had some very considerable

M

qualities. He had great perseverance, never wasted his time, and whatever special matter he had in hand, would return to his occupation in every interval of leisure from his ordinary pursuits. He had great sagacity, and was never deterred from any undertaking which he had once begun by the difficulties which he met with. What I said of him in my Hunterian Oration in the year 1837, I believe to present a just view of his professional character: 'He was a great practical surgeon. His mind went directly to the leading points of the case before him, disregarding all those minor points by which minds of smaller capacity are perplexed and misled. Hence his views of disease were clear, and such as were easily communicated to his pupils; and his practice was simple and decided. He never shrank from difficulties, but, on the contrary, seemed to have pleasure in meeting them and overcoming them; and I am satisfied that to this one of his qualities many of his patients were indebted for their lives. Much valuable information may be found in his surgical works, and his observations on Ulcers and on Diseases of the Prostate Gland may be perused with advantage by the best-educated surgeons of the present day.'

Having been educated in John Hunter's Museum, he was at the earliest period of his professional life initiated in the pursuit of comparative anatomy, and he never relinquished it even during those years in which he was most occupied with his practice as a surgeon. This led to his associating on terms of the greatest intimacy with Sir Joseph Banks (over whom he had great influence), and others of that constellation of great men who were at that time ornaments of the Royal Society. His early papers on Anatomy, published in the 'Philosophical Transactions,' are of great and acknowledged value. But, unfortunately for his reputation, his ambition rather increased than diminished, while his mental powers were gradually declining under the influence of gout and increasing years. In his latter days he had an overweening desire to appear before the world as a discoverer; and his friends in the Council of the Royal Society too readily admitted whatever he offered them into the Society's Transactions; and the result has been, that many of his later communications are of such a nature that his best friends found reason to regret that they were published.

Some years before he died, he got great discredit from having destroyed a considerable portion of John Hunter's manuscripts, which had come into his possession as one of Hunter's executors. This act was equally unjustifiable and foolish. It was unjustifiable, because the manuscripts should have been considered as belonging to the Museum, which Parliament had purchased; and it was foolish, because it has led to the notion that he had made use of John Hunter's observations for his own purposes, much more than was really the case. I had frequent opportunities of seeing these papers during nine or ten years in which I was accustomed, more or less, conjointly with Clift, to assist him in his dissections. They consisted of rough notes on the anatomy of animals, which must have been useful to Hunter himself, and which would, I doubt not, have afforded help to Mr. Owen in completing the Catalogue of the

Museum; but they were not such as could be used with much advantage by another person. In pursuing his own investigations Home sometimes referred to them, but I must say that while I was connected with him I never knew an instance in which he did not scrupulously acknowledge whatever he took from them, and do justice to his illustrious predecessor. Unhappily, he was led afterwards to deviate from this right course, and in his later publications I recognize some things which he has given as the result of his own observation, though they were really taken from Hunter's notes and drawings. One of these is a paper on the progressive motion of animals, and another a series of engravings representing the convolutions of the intestinal canal, and neither of them of much scientific value. When the Duke of Cumberland had been wounded by Sellis in the attempt to assassinate him, he attended the Duke in Carlton House. This circumstance first introduced him to the Prince Regent. The Prince found his society agreeable, and used to invite him frequently to dinner, treating him with much familiarity.

In the year 1834 the King was pleased to elevate me to the rank of a baronet. I cannot say that this had ever been any great object of ambition with me, yet from the way it was done I could not but feel gratified by the honour conferred on me. I have in my possession a letter from my friend General Sir Charles Thornton, who was one of his Majesty's equerries, stating that a person who was much in King William's confidence (I conclude it was Sir Herbert Taylor) had informed him that the King had said to him that it was his intention to make me a baronet, though not quite immediately. It was one or two years afterwards, when Lord Grey was quitting his office as prime minister, being succeeded by Lord Melbourne, that Lord Brougham said to me, 'You ought to be a baronet, and I know that Lord Grey intends to speak to the King on the subject, though it has escaped his memory to do so.' At that time my income, derived from my savings, and independent of my practice, did not amount to more than about £2500 or £2000 per annum; and I thought that the being a baronet would not add very greatly to my own importance, while it might, in the event of my death, rather hamper my elder son. I expressed this to Lord Brougham, and said I should prefer to wait until I had acquired more landed property, and such as any one having anything in the shape of hereditary rank ought to be able to bequeath to his family. Being, however, at the moment pressed for time, I added that I would speak to him again on the subject.   When I saw him on the following day, I was about to repeat my former observations, when he interrupted me by saying, ' It is too late now to think about it— Lord Melbourne applied to the King yesterday, who immediately assented, and the thing is settled ; ' and so a baronet I became. This change in my condition, however really unimportant in itself, and however small in the eyes of mere aristocratic persons, considerably affected my views and plans as to the future. Prosperous as I was in my profession, I had always felt that I was overworked, and that what I gained in income was counterbalanced by the loss of comfort. It had been my dream (it would, I doubt not, have proved only a dream) that I would, when I had made some further provision for my family, retire from professional practice, and resume my former pursuits in physiology. But now the case was altered. An hereditary rank, however small, without some independent fortune, is really an incumbrance, and I considered it rather as a duty to those who were to come after me not to leave them in this situation. Thus I was led to persevere in my former course; and it was not until three or four years afterwards that, by affording myself a long vacation during the summer and autumn, I obtained any considerable relaxation from my labours.

In the year 1834 I succeeded to the first vacancy that occurred, after my being appointed serjeant-surgeon, in the Court of Examiners of the College of Surgeons. I did so not by election, but under the provisions of the charter in virtue of my office as serjeant-surgeon. The original object of this arrangement was, I suppose, that two responsible servants of the Crown should belong to the court, instead of it being altogether nominated by the college. In this

way Sir David Dundas, who was not at the time
even a member of the college, had become one
of the examiners about forty years previously.
The business of examining young men who are
candidates for admission into a profession becomes after some time very irksome; the same-
ness and tediousness of it being in this instance
very little compensated by the moderate pecuniary advantages which belong to it. When a
new charter was granted to the college some
years afterwards, establishing the order of Fellows, by whom the council were to be elected,
and requiring the bye-laws to be submitted to
and sanctioned by the Secretary of State, the
rule as to the serjeant-surgeons being *ex-officio*
members of the Court of Examiners was dispensed with, and I availed myself of this opportunity to resign my office as an examiner.

Under the original charter of the college,
none but members of the council were eligible
to the Court of Examiners, and they were very
generally elected according to seniority. There
was, however, no absolute rule on the subject;
and I remember one occasion on which three

councillors (no one of whom certainly would
have been competent as examiner) were passed
over in succession, to elect Lawrence, as to
whose qualifications there could be no difference
of opinion.   The monopoly of the examinership
by the council had always been considered as
a grievance, and the more so as the examiners
received a certain income as the reward of their
services.   Yet I cannot say that any real harm
resulted from it.   At the time of my being an
examiner, there was only one of my colleagues
who had not been a hospital surgeon, and he
had been a teacher of anatomy; so that at any
rate they had had the opportunity of being qualified for their duties.   As to practical surgery,
I do not conceive there could have been any
much better selection, the examiners being all
men who had a large share of professional experience, and such as could not have been found
among younger men.   In anatomy the examination might have been improved.   It was conducted altogether *vivâ voce*, except in osteology.
It would certainly have been difficult to procure
a regular weekly supply of subjects throughout

the year for examination by dissection; but a good deal more might have been done then, and might be done now, by requiring the candidates to describe what they saw in preserved specimens of natural structure, and in those exhibiting the changes produced by disease.   The great objection to the *vivâ voce* examination is the facility with which a student, having a good memory and a clever tutor, may qualify himself for the ordeal by cramming.   This was. done then, and is done still to a frightful extent.   The same objection does not apply to the examination in practical surgery when conducted by *well-informed and experienced* surgeons.   My own view of the matter is, that while hospital surgeons somewhat advanced in their profession should be the principal element in a court of examiners, it will be well to have conjoined with them a certain number of younger men, fresh from their anatomical studies, who, not being much engaged in practice, would have more leisure to bestow on the anatomical part of the examination than the elders of the profession.

It would also be a great improvement on the

present system if the examination were conducted at two distinct periods ; the one relating
to anatomy and physiology taking place when
half the period allotted to education was expired, and the other at the termination of the
whole. Further, without giving up the *vivâ
voce* examination altogether, a part of the examination should be always conducted by means
of written papers. I own that I think very
little of an objection which has been made to
the examinations at the college, that they are
not sufficiently extensive. It is to be observed
that the objects of the examination for the
membership of the College of Surgeons is merely
to ascertain whether the candidate has that
minimum of knowledge, without which it would
not be safe for any one to commence practice,
and which, if he has sufficient opportunities and
industry, and powers of observation, may enable
him after some time to become a good and useful practitioner. The first requisite for a good
examination is, *that there should be good examiners.* One who is well qualified for the task
will seldom fail, in the course of half an hour,

to ascertain whether the candidate has made good use of his time as a student; while another, less qualified, who has to prepare himself for the occasion, may persevere in the examination for many hours, and blunder at last.

I may take this opportunity of observing that it is a great mistake to compare the examination of young men entering a profession with those for degrees in a university. A senior wrangler may be a great mathematician, and a first-class man in classics may be a first-rate Greek scholar; but the utmost that can be expected of a young lawyer, or physician, or surgeon is, that he should show that he has laid such a foundation as may enable him to profit by the opportunities of experience which may be presented to him afterwards. To be a thorough master of his profession in the beginning of his career is out of the question, and is a thing to be attained only by unremitting study and close observation, continued during a long series of years.

The above remarks do not exactly apply to the examination for the Fellowship of the college. The object of this institution is to ensure the introduction into the profession of a certain number of young men who may be qualified to maintain its scientific character, and will be fully equal to its higher duties as hospital surgeons, teachers, and improvers of physiological, pathological, and surgical science afterwards. With this view, if they have not university degrees, they are required to undergo a preliminary examination in classics and mathematics ; while, their professional education having been continued for a longer period of time, they are expected to show that they have a more perfect acquaintance with those sciences which are the foundation of medical and surgical knowledge than can be expected of the great majority of those who are candidates for practice. If this system be properly and honestly carried out, I apprehend that the result will be that the Fellowship of the College of Surgeons will be the most honourable distinction that is offered to the junior members of the medical profession.

For several years during this period of my

life I find little as regards myself that is worthy of being recorded. With my constant professional engagements, and being from time to time engaged in writing and in preparing successive editions of my books, it may well be supposed that I had little leisure to attend to other pursuits. The circumstances in which I was placed necessarily brought me in contact with a great number and variety of persons of all grades in society, and from all quarters of the globe; and there was much to interest me in the various phases of human nature that were thus presented to my observation; but this is no more than what happens to all those who have any large dealings with mankind. Either personally, or by correspondence in writing, there were few members of my own profession with whom I was not more or less in communication; but such communications were of course more frequent with those who, like myself, were in extensive practice in London; and of these I feel it rather a duty to say that I found them almost uniformly obliging and accommodating, liberal-minded, and more free from petty jealousies than could be well expected of any body of men who were competing for reputation in the same pursuit. Sir Astley Cooper was still nominally in practice, and I frequently called him into consultation in cases in which either my patients or myself were desirous of having a second opinion : but he was chiefly occupied with anatomical researches, and in making a collection of preparations, which, after his death, was purchased of his nephew, Mr. Bransby Cooper, by the College of Surgeons. For some years after the death of King George IV., Sir Henry Halford retained the largest practice as a physician. The necessary result of the positions which we occupied in our respective departments was that I was in more frequent communication with him than with any other member of the medical profession. He was a clever and sagacious physician, with a great deal of practical information, but without any of that scientific knowledge which is necessary for a right diagnosis of disease. He was on the whole a very useful and successful practitioner; but his views of disease were limited, and he was too apt to be contented with relieving the present symptoms, instead of tracing them to their origin, and making it his object to remove the cause which produced them. He was a good Latin scholar, and prided himself rather over-much on his skill in composing Latin verses. From being in frequent attendance on the Royal Family, with whom he was a favourite, he had acquired too much of the habits and feelings of a courtier. Still, he was in many respects an ornament of his profession, and was a worthy representative of it as President of the College of Physicians.

At this time his most successful competitor was my intimate friend (and colleague at St. George's Hospital) Dr. Chambers. He was a thorough gentleman in the best sense of the word, an accomplished scholar, and had been a diligent student in his profession. Although Sir Henry Halford continued to be in attendance on King William, the Queen seemed to prefer Dr. Chambers's straightforwardness to the

. N

courtier-like manners of the other. Latterly Chambers was consulted by the King himself, and he was in attendance on his Majesty during his last illness, in conjunction with Sir David Davis, the King's domestic physician. From this time Dr. Chambers had the largest share of medical practice in the metropolis, and he well merited the estimation in which he was held by both the public and the members of his own profession. But his physical powers were scarcely equal to the labours which were thus imposed on him. One forenoon, when I was occupied in seeing patients at my own house, he called on me in a state of considerable alarm, having been suddenly affected with a difficulty of articulation. This attack was not of long duration. But it was the first symptom of a disease of the brain, which, though for a long time impercep- tible to others, was too plain to those who were intimately acquainted with him, and which caused his death several years afterwards. He had purchased a house with a small estate on the sea-coast in Hampshire, to which, when no longer in a fit state to pursue his profession, he retired, and where he passed the few remaining years of his life. Chambers had an extensive knowledge of his profession, and his great natural sagacity enabled him readily to apply what he knew to the investigation and treatment of the cases which were presented to him. He was altogether an excellent practitioner, but he never ventured to communicate the result of his observations to the public, and thus has left nothing behind him by which he will be known in the next generation. But the same thing may be said of many others. The best part of the knowledge which the ablest practitioners have acquired dies with them; and the rule applies even to those whose names are preserved to us by their written works. It is only a small part of the experience of Sydenham, or Pott, or Hunter, that has been really transmitted to posterity. They may have set up certain landmarks to guide us in our course, but the multitude of smaller details on which success in practice mainly depends are, for the most part, not of a nature to be transmitted in writing.

I had been, from the earliest part of my professional career, in one way or another, so much occupied that I had never found leisure, until after what may be regarded as the middle period of my life, to visit the Continent. In the year 1837 I paid my first visit to Paris, remaining there for a month, having previously made a tour in Normandy with Lady Brodie and our daughter. I had formerly become acquainted with several persons of eminence in that metropolis when they visited London, especially with Cuvier, Orfila, Blainville, Roux, Edwards, Magendie, and Paul Dubois. I had seen Dupuytren only on one occasion, when he came to London to be present at the marriage of one of the family of the Rothschilds. At the time at which I am now writing, the only one of these that remains is Dubois. I was received with great kindness by my former friends and by others whom I had not known before. Since .then, up to the present time (1857), except in passing through it in my way elsewhere, I have paid only one visit to the French metropolis; and I have been only once in Switzerland, and once in Italy as far as Milan.

As a boy I had read a good deal of both French and Italian, and I have been in the constant habit of reading French ever since.   But in the early part of my life there was so little intercourse with foreigners, that the opportunities of conversing with them were of rare occurrence; and when they did occur, after the termination of the long war, I was so entirely occupied by my other pursuits, that I did not avail myself sufficiently of them.   The consequence has been that, although I read French as easily as English, I have never acquired the habit of speaking it with facility; and this is probably one reason why I have felt less inclination to travel on the Continent than I should have felt otherwise.   It is worthy of notice that formerly the speaking French was far from being a frequent accomplishment.   Sir Joseph Banks never conversed with foreigners without the aid of an interpreter, and I have understood that Mr. Canning did not acquire the habit of speaking French until he was, as it were, compelled to do so by becoming the Secretary of State for the Foreign Department.

During the more active period of my professional life I was never absent from London for more than a few weeks in the year. In the year 1828 I engaged a house on Hampstead Heath, which at that time was a comparatively rural retreat. My family resided there during the summer and part of the autumnal season, and I generally was able to go thither to dinner, returning to my occupation in London in the morning. My lease having nearly expired, in the year 1837 I purchased the property which I now have in Surrey, with a larger and more convenient residence. Although I was never confined by illness, except on two or three occasions for a few days at a time, yet I had rarely enjoyed the feeling of being in perfect health. In fact, I was scarcely strong enough for the work which I had to do, and I have little doubt that my health would have failed altogether, if it had not been that my labours were made lighter by the consciousness of success, and that long experience had made me so familiar with the practice of my profession, that few things which were presented to me required any painful effort of mind to enable me to understand them. The time had now arrived when it seemed reasonable that I should consult my own comfort by some relaxation from my former exertions. Although we had lived with little regard to expense, yet the considerable income which my profession afforded me, had enabled me to make such a provision for my family and myself, that I had no further anxiety on this account. I had never been oppressed by the desire to accumulate a fortune, beyond that which was required to prevent my wife and children from " going down in the world" in the event of my being taken from them; and in establishing myself in my new residence in Surrey, I at once determined to retire to it during a considerable part of the summer and autumn, and to extend my vacation annually. To this plan I have faithfully adhered, and I have every reason to be satisfied with the result. Having the advantage of some kind and intelligent neighbours, being visited by some of my early friends, whom I had little opportunity of seeing at other times, and always taking with me some work to be done, either in preparing a new edition of one of my books, or in some other way, I have never experienced any kind of inconvenience from the want of occupation. I have no taste for what are called country pursuits, in shooting or hunting. For some years I tried that of farming, but I was not long enough in the country to take any great interest in it, nor much to understand it; and as I found that it afforded me little amusement to counterbalance the pecuniary loss which it occasioned, I prudently abandoned this new undertaking. I have always devoted a portion of the time which I passed in the country, to the renewal of some of the studies of my early life. But if I had trusted to this alone, I am convinced that my new mode of life would not have added to my happiness. It must be confessed that to those who have been long accustomed to the active pursuits of life, and the variety and excitement belonging to them, mere reading and learning is but dull work, and quite insufficient to prevent the miseries of *ennui*, and the degradation of mind which *ennui* necessarily produces.

In March, 1808, I was elected Assistant-Surgeon to St. George's Hospital. In January, 1840, after having filled the place of assistant-surgeon for fourteen years, and that of surgeon for nearly eighteen years, I resigned my office. During these thirty-two years the hospital, as far as my profession was concerned, was the greatest object of interest that I possessed. Except during the brief intervals of my absence from London, it rarely happened that I was not some time during the day within its walls. I was indebted to the opportunities which it afforded me for the best part of the knowledge which I had been able to attain. It had rendered my professional life one of agreeable study, instead of one of mechanical and irksome drudgery. Some of my happiest hours were those during which I was occupied in the wards, with my pupils around me, answering their enquiries, explaining the cases to them at the bedside of the patients, informing them as to the grounds on which I formed my diagnosis, and my reasons for the treatment which I employed, and not concealing from them my oversights and

o

errors; and all this to kind and willing and only too partial listeners. My intercourse with the students, and, I may add, with the patients also, was always to me a source of real gratification; and even now (many years afterwards) these scenes are often renewed to me at night, and events of which I have no recollection when awake come before me in my dreams. It was not without a painful effort that I made up my mind to resign an office to which I had been sincerely attached. In doing so I was influenced by various considerations. One of them was that I began to feel the necessity of diminishing the amount of my labours. Then I had long since formed the resolution that I would not have it said of myself, as I had heard it said of others, that I retained a situation of such importance and responsibility when, either from age or from indifference, I had ceased to be fully equal to the duties belonging to it; and lastly, when I saw intelligent and diligent and otherwise deserving young men around me, waiting their turn to succeed to the hospital appointments, it seemed to me that there was something selfish in standing longer in their way, when, as far as my own mere worldly interests were concerned, I had obtained all that I could desire. I have found no reason to be dissatisfied with the resolution which I had formed, and the step which I took in consequence; yet, for some considerable time after I had taken it, I had many uncomfortable feelings, and I never passed by the hospital without something like a painful recollection that my labours there were at an end. However, I kept up in some degree my connection with it for some years after my resignation, by delivering annually a short course of lectures gratuitously to the students during the winter session, generally selecting for that purpose some one class of diseases, giving a more detailed history of my own experience than it was possible to give in an ordinary course of surgical lectures.

PRINTED BY SPOTTISWOODE AND CO., NEW-STREET SQUARE, LONDON

www.ingramcontent.com/pod-product-compliance
Lightning Source LLC
Chambersburg PA
CBHW031106020726

47495CB00007B/2064